The Disappearance of Olivia

NANCY E. RYAN

DEDICATION

This Book is dedicated in memory of my mother Doris who showed me the way by example and to my father Bill who was the most courageous man that I have ever known.

ACKNOWLEDGMENTS

The Disappearance of Olivia would not have been possible without the support and unconditional love of my husband Barry, my daughter Melissa, and her husband Ricardo. I can't thank you enough. I love you. Anyone who knows me understands that I am a conceptual person – a great dreamer of stories – not a writer. Thank god I found Alan Forray.

Alan is a gifted writer who has helped me materialize the life of Olivia through his talent.

Noreen, thank you so very much for your friendship. You are exceptional. Cousin Christine your help has been immeasurable. Luke, thank you my gifted nephew for keeping me in the "now". Lucia, thank you for encouraging me to get Olivia's story told, and for the strategic 'kick in the pants' not to mention all your hours of support and interest. Helen, you were the first to hear about Olivia. Thank you for lending me your British ears, face and voice. Sue thank you for getting involved with another "Nancy Project". Your help is greatly appreciated. My experts in online marketing, New Epic Media thank you for everything.

SUCCESSION

Succession in the United Kingdom is governed by the Act of Union 1800, which restates the provisions of the Act of Settlement 1701 and the Bill of Rights 1689. Only Protestant heirs of Princess Sophia, Neither Catholics nor those who marry a Catholic, nor those born out of wedlock, may remain in the line of succession.

The current Royal Line of Succession is:

Prince Charles

Prince William

Prince Henry

Or is it?

IN VITRO FERTILIZATION

In Vitro Fertilization (IVF) is the process by which eggs are retrieved from a woman's ovary and fertilized by sperm outside the body. The fertilized egg (zygote), in a few days is then transferred into the patient's uterus. This procedure was first successful with the birth of Louise Brown, born July 25, 1978, in, Oldham General Hospital, Oldham, and Greater Manchester, UK).

"I want to walk into a room, be it a hospital for the dying or a hospital for the sick children, and feel that I am needed. I want to do, not just to be."

—Diana, Princess of Wales

The Disappearance of Olivia

NANCY E. RYAN
with ALAN FORRAY

THE DISAPPEARANCE OF OLIVIA

Copyright © 2011 by Nancy E. Ryan

Library of Congress Cataloging-in-Publication Data

Available upon request

This is a work of fiction. All of the characters, organizations and events portrayed in this novel are either products of the author's imagination or are used fictitiously.

The Disappearance of Olivia

Cover design by Erika R. Decker

ISBN-13: 978-1463794125

ISBN-10: 1463794126

Chapter One

March 5, 2011

The mob of staff and patients on the eighth floor of John Radcliffe Hospital looked more like the January Super Sale at Harrods than the corridor of the cutting-edge medical facility that the Oxford Radcliffe Hospitals were trying to promote to the public. The fact that Radcliffe was one of the premier teaching hospitals in the United Kingdom did not negate the fact that healthcare worldwide was experiencing a growing crisis in funding and recruitment. Perhaps it was the 7:00 a.m. shift change, or the onslaught of medical students who were there for morning rounds, or maybe it was the large tray of muffins and crumpets at the nurses' station; whatever the case, the shoulder-to-shoulder crowd of white coats that jammed the hallway might just as well have been packed together in the Tube at rush hour.

Standing head and shoulders above the rest was Dr. Olivia Victoria Franklin, a stunning 5'10" woman with shoulder length blonde hair and killer legs, who was finishing up a dual residency in oncology and hematology as part of her specialization in childhood leukemia at the Childhood Cancer Research Group at Oxford. Just as her father, Dr. Arthur Franklin, had done, Olivia went to Oxford both as an undergraduate student in science and later as a medical student. Her mother, Elizabeth Franklin, had also taught at Oxford for a time as a professor of archeology and anthropology.

As Olivia trudged slowly down the corridor, she received the usual admiring glances from onlookers who never seemed to get enough of that "special something" she seemed to exude. A classic beauty with a brilliant smile and eyes that seemed to add an iridescent glow to the dull mauve walls of the hospital, Olivia was a glowing star with an indescribable aura about her and a resplendent future that would likely extend well beyond her scientific acumen.

Almost at the bank of elevators at the end of the corridor, Olivia caught a glimpse of Dr. Daniel Whittemore who was at the nurses' station focusing all his attention on the enormous pastry tray. Daniel was Olivia's first love and the man who broke her heart. Although their relationship was long over, he always took her breath away when she would see him. Eight years her senior, Daniel was dreamy...6'2", 180 lbs. both athletic and fit, with short black hair and large brown eyes that reflected both his genius and passion. Daniel was now one of her colleagues at Oxford and running into him was unavoidable. She paused for a moment, hoping to make eye contact with the distinguished pediatric intensivist. Today, his eyes never left the pastries and the crumpets won out.

Making her way to within a few feet of the elevators, her thoughts consumed with Daniel, she was suddenly, and quite violently, thrust into an empty patient room and slammed face forward against a wall. As she struggled to free herself from her unseen attacker, she barely saw the hypodermic needle being pressed into the side of her neck. A moment later, the walls of the room went from mauve to black.

It was Daniel Whittemore who was first doctor on the scene, along with a number of nurses. It was the same Dr. Whittemore who immediately recognized the symptoms of anaphylaxis, but he knew that something more was going on.

Olivia was exhibiting faint, high-pitched, intermittent breathing sounds, dangerously low blood pressure, cardiac arrhythmia, and blueness of the skin, with the rapid appearance of hives all over her body. She was also convulsing and starting to foam at the mouth. Her face was becoming cyanosed with dilated pupils and prominent eyeballs. Within moments, Olivia was being "bagged" to assist her breathing, placed on an IV, and given a hefty dose of epinephrine.

By the time she was moved downstairs, the ER was almost as crowded as the eighth floor corridor. Between the emergency room doctors, nurses, a consulting cardiologist, a pulmonologist, and Dr. Whittemore, there was barely room to maneuver around the IV racks, the respirator, and the EKG. Had it not been for an orderly sent to prep the empty patient room just moments after Olivia's collapse, the shouts of "code blue" and the immediate administration of CPR would have come too late.

Within minutes of Olivia arriving in ER 5, the real work began. A gaggle of senior emergency room doctors and nurses were intermingled with a small group of internists and other specialists who had swooped into the unit the moment they learned of Olivia's critical condition. Standing in a corner trying to remain unobtrusive was Daniel Whittemore and his favorite nurse practitioner, Margaret Osborne, who was dutifully entering every event into the notepad computer that had recently replaced their clipboards and paper charts. Margaret had worked with Dr. Whittemore for years, and he sometimes thought she knew more about medicine than he did. Margaret observed that Olivia was being administered intravenous anticonvulsants along with muscle relaxants.

As the two of them stared at the display of Olivia's vital signs, the tangle of tubes that ran to both arms, the slow beeping of the respirator, and the ultrasound that was being performed on the patient's liver and kidneys, all they could do was watch, wait, and pray that the lab would soon come back with the tox screen of Olivia's blood work.

It had probably been fewer than ten minutes from the time Olivia was found to the moment at hand, but it already seemed to Daniel Whittemore that hours had elapsed. Such is too often the case with severely critical patients...time runs out.

It was a resident Whittemore was training who suddenly moved from Olivia's bedside, walked to the corner where Whittemore and Osborne where standing, and discreetly urged the two of them to join him in the hallway outside the room. On the way out the door, Osborne handed off her digital chart to one of her colleagues.

"So what do you think, John?" Whittemore asked his protégé. "Could this be a severe allergic reaction?"

"More than that," the resident said ominously. "Much more, I'm afraid."

Over the next few minutes, the resident, John Wolsey, told Whittemore and Osborne that, after brushing aside Olivia's hair to check her carotid pulse, he had noticed a small droplet of blood, which appeared to have come from an injection in her neck.

"This was deliberate?" Whittemore gasped.

"I can see no other reasonable explanation," Wolsey answered. "Either someone did this to her, or . . ." he let his answer trail off.

"Self- inflicted?" Whittemore came back, noticeably shocked and incredulous. "Not Olivia, never!"

"Impossible!" said Nurse Osborne. "Olivia is one of my best friends and I know her! She is so filled with life, joy, hope, optimism—she couldn't have done this in a million years. For god's sake! I see her every day. I saw her two minutes before this happened! Impossible!"

"I have to tell you, John," Whittemore continued, "I know Olivia pretty damn well, more than that, actually, and I can tell you with one hundred percent certainty that Olivia did not do this to herself."

They all just stared at one another for several moments as the only logical explanation set in. Someone wants Olivia dead.

A little bit after ten that morning, the preliminary toxicology report came in. Olivia's blood contained a massive dose of penicillin, along with traces of strychnine. The two drugs working in unison had put Olivia into a deep coma, though now that the doctors knew what they were dealing with, her prospects for recovery were not so bleak.

At 10:00 that evening, the decision was made to transfer the patient from emergency to intensive care. Dr. Whittemore and Nurse Osborne would handle the transfer, along with two security guards who were personally known to them.

At precisely 10:55 p.m., just minutes ahead of the evening shift change, Dr. Olivia Franklin, still unconscious on a gurney, was wheeled to the elevator for her trip to the fourth floor I.C.U. After ensuring that the elevator contained no other occupants and using a key that would allow them to move to their floor with no stops in between, Dr. Whittemore glanced at the escorts, who gave him a nod.

He then looked at Olivia, still beautiful in her sleep, and pressed the button that would take them to the basement and the awaiting ambulance.

Chapter Two

The drive from Oxford to Central London takes little more than an hour, unless, of course, the driver and all his passengers are so profoundly concerned that they take the most circuitous route imaginable.

Behind the wheel of the ambulance was John Parker; a stalwart built 30 year-old who looked more like a forward on a rugby team than a hospital security guard. In the passenger seat to his left was Guy Devon, 20 years John's senior, a retired member of the MPS (Metropolitan Police Service) whom Daniel Whittemore had known for years.

It was a risky business transporting Olivia in her precarious condition; then again, so was attempted murder, a thought shared by all the passengers.

"Here it is," said Nurse Osborne, who was tapping on her notepad computer. "Extremely hyper-allergenic . . . bee stings, certain foods—especially peanuts—and penicillin."

Without a word, Dr. Whittemore pulled out his cell phone.

"Donnie, it's me . . . yeah, we're fine and en route. Listen, I think you should try to get a hold of Eddie and have him meet us at the clinic immediately. Tell him to keep it under his hat, if that's possible with that fat head of his. For the time being, we need to keep this under wraps. Okay, see you soon."

Osborne looked up from her notebook and gazed inquisitively into Whittemore's eyes. "You do know what you're doing, right?" she inquired with a noticeable tone of doubt in her voice.

Whittemore paused and massaged his brow.

"Haven't a clue, my dear."

"So what else is new?" she said and returned to her computer files.

The ambulance finally arrived at 20 Devonshire Place W1, home of London Acute Care. It was met at the Emergency entrance of the Critical Care Unit, world-renowned for diagnosing and treating conditions that other medical facilities found particularly problematic.

Standing on the loading dock were Dr. Donald Glynne, the director of the clinic, and Chief Inspector Edward Armstrong of Scotland Yard.

After some hearty hugs between Whittemore and the other two, perfunctory introductions were made to Osborne and the security guards, and then Olivia was moved from the ambulance to the clinic.

After settling Olivia into a private room directly across from the tenth floor nurses' station, preliminary instructions were given to the private nurse at Olivia's bedside, and the rest of the entourage adjourned to a nearby conference room.

"Hey, Guy!" Chief Inspector Armstrong said to the former RMP Major, whom he recognized from a joint operation they had once worked involving a missing Major Cadet.

"I'm flattered you remember me, sir," Devon responded. "We only worked together for a couple of weeks."

"I don't forget much, my friend . . . with the exception of my wife's birthday and most holidays."

A few knowing eye rolls all around, but then the Chief Inspector was suddenly all business, taking charge of the meeting, as he was quite accustomed to doing.

"So what's this all about, Danny?" he said to his friend.

Truth be told, Danny, Eddie, and Donnie had been fast friends since their prep school days at Ripley Court in Surrey. As eleven year-olds, they'd made a blood pact that they would stand together, come what may, for the whole of their lives. Thus far, that had mostly consisted of sharing a few pints at St. Stephen's Tavern from time to time.

As Dr. Whittemore recounted the events of the day, Chief Inspector Armstrong took copious notes, as was his practice. At one point John Parker interrupted, saying that he'd feel more comfortable up on the tenth floor, outside Olivia's room.

"Better you should stay inside with the nurse," Armstrong suggested. "We don't want to raise any suspicions."

Parker nodded and left the room.

While the remaining assemblage went over and over every last detail of the day, things became a bit more directed, as Chief Inspector Armstrong would frequently interrupt with questions:

Are you aware of any enemies she may have had?

A jilted suitor?

A disgruntled co-worker?

An irate parent of one of her patients?

Someone from her past she may have mentioned?

A controversial cause she was involved in?

Anyone suspicious hanging around the ward?

A jealous boyfriend?

A jealous girlfriend?

Anyone who seemed to be taking a particular interest in her?

Nothing. All they knew at that point was that someone had done this to Olivia.

"So, what's your theory, Sherlock?" Whittemore asked the detective after going round and round for hours.

"Well, as Sir Arthur Conan Doyle himself was fond of saying, 'It's a mystery to me.'"

Whittemore pushed back his chair, leaped to his feet, "So, what now?" he shouted. "Where do we go from here?"

"Sit down, Danny," his friend said casually. "Now, we make a plan."

Chapter Three

They were sitting in a corner of the hospital cafeteria—just Danny, Eddie, Donnie, and Margaret. Guy had taken the ambulance back to Radcliffe, and John was still upstairs in Olivia's room with the private nurse.

"So, what's the plan?" Nurse Osborne was the first to ask.

The Chief Inspector turned to Danny and paused thoughtfully before he spoke.

"Have you ever met Olivia's parents?" he asked the doctor.

"A number of times," he answered. "A couple of social events at the hospital, and once for a dinner party at their home. Olivia and I were involved for a time."

"OK. First things first. You need to go to the Franklin's home and tell them what has happened. You can't call them because, A: The phones may not be secure, and B: 'cause that's a damn shitty way to deliver news such as this."

"You're right, of course," Whittemore said and started to rise from his seat.

"Not so fast, Danny." He took a deep breath and then continued speaking.

"Olivia's parents are going to want to get here as quickly as possible. That's a given. What I need you to do is to take a cab from London Acute Care around the houses by way of Bombay, Paris, and the Ukraine, and bring the Franklins back here in a similar fashion, with no one who might be trying to tag along and do it within an hour."

"Do you really think this is such an elaborate threat that we have to go to such lengths?"

"Just say it's my gut feeling," he said.

"Well you certainly have the gut to work with!" Daniel laughing as he headed for the door.

"Make fun all you want, I am going to make sure that Olivia is safe," Armstrong snapped back at his friend.

The trip to Knightsbridge was largely uneventful; save for a brief stop at the Hackney terminal, where a hundred black, Austin taxis came and went every few minutes.

Throughout the ride, the thoughts in Daniel Whittemore's head were racing like thoroughbreds at Ascot:

Why would someone want to kill Olivia?

Why in the hospital where she would receive immediate care?

Why with such a crowd about when he or she could easily have been spotted?

Could this have been an inside job?

How can we protect her if someone wants her dead?

Why am I talking to myself?

Daniel folded himself into the comfy back seat of the Austin and tried to quiet his mind.

He began with a deep breathing exercise in which he visualized cleansing energy entering through his nose and negative energy exhaled through his mouth.

After about a minute of this, he slowly altered his visualization so that the air he was breathing was a golden-white light that painlessly passed through the crest of his skull and travelled slowly through his brain to his neck and face. With every inhalation after that, the comforting light, which was the breath of the universe, traveled down his body, to his shoulders, along his spine, to every organ of his abdomen, down through his hips, his legs, and finally to his feet.

It didn't work for shit.

When they got to the Franklins, the driver circled the block. Then they parked down the street, where Daniel made his way to the door of their home, ever vigilant all the while.

Knightsbridge is a rather exclusive area of West London that runs along the south side of Hyde Park. In a class-conscious society such as England, one naturally assumes that its residents are upper crust.

After pretty much barging in on the Franklins and announcing the purpose of his visit, Daniel tried as best he could to reassure them that Olivia was receiving the finest care available anywhere.

Not sure they were really listening, he watched as Olivia's parents grabbed coats and hats and made their way outside where the taxi was now waiting.

On the ride to London Acute Care, Dr. Daniel Whittemore did his best to explain Olivia's medical condition. Not wanting to alarm them anymore than they already were, he skipped a few details.

"She's going to be fine," he assured them.

"The same thing happened when she was six," said Elizabeth Franklin. "Bloody bee sting, it was. Good thing I was there to pull out the stinger and use that EpiPen thingy. What a dreadful thing to have to live with," she sighed.

"Hey! This isn't the way to Radcliffe," Arthur Franklin suddenly exclaimed. "What in the heck is going on here?"

"Now, now, Arthur. I'm sure Daniel has a perfectly good explanation for this," said his wife, gently patting her husband's hand. "An explanation he is about to give us in full detail," she added sternly. "Isn't that right, Daniel?"

Back at Oxford Radcliffe, there were now more people wearing custodian helmets than white hospital garb.

When Olivia was first discovered passed out on the floor, nobody called 999 Emergency—they were, after all, in a hospital.

Such was not the case at 11:40 that evening, when Olivia was clearly missing and all the staff were beside themselves.

First on the scene and in charge of the investigation was Detective Nigel Prescott, the reigning darts champion at a dozen pubs around London, including St. Stephen's Tavern.

Chief Inspector Armstrong had called him even before the folks at Radcliffe filed their missing persons report with the Thames Valley Police, and Nigel had already been assigned to liaise with the TVP. Though it would cost Chief Inspector Armstrong the kinds of favors usually associated with an arm and a leg, Nigel was keeping the investigation focused on the missing patient and nothing else.

Also receiving a call that evening, this one from Daniel, was Dr. John Wolsey, the resident who had told Daniel and Margaret about the droplet of blood on Olivia's neck and the apparent injection that had caused it. He too was not blabbing about an attempted murder, but in ER5 he did inform the attending physicians about the strychnine poisoning and made sure Olivia received a dose of charcoal, the only known treatment for strychnine poisoning. He had also made it clear to all the attending doctors and nurses that word from the senior leadership was to say nothing about the "potential" poisoning—no need to cause a panic.

When the Franklins finally arrived at Olivia's room in London Acute Care, they were aghast at seeing all the tubes and equipment attached to their daughter. Elizabeth Franklin immediately broke down, sobbing profusely on her husband's shoulder.

"It's not as bad as it looks," the attending physician said to Daniel, who for the past ninety minutes had been monitoring Olivia's condition.

"Her vitals are near normal, the latest blood work is excellent; she's responding well to treatment."

"So why is she in a coma?" Arthur Franklin asked Daniel. Dr. Arthur Franklin was just a worried father and wasn't even thinking like a physician.

Whittemore paused and took a deep breath before he spoke.

"Arthur, Elizabeth, your daughter has just been through an extremely traumatic event. Believe me. Everything that modern medicine is capable of is being brought to bear."

No one said anything for a long, lingering moment; then Elizabeth Franklin moved to her daughter's bed and gently sat by her side.

"My sweet baby, I don't know if you can hear me, but please understand that everything will be okay. Your father and I both love you very much, and your friends and colleagues will not let you down. By all that is holy, I swear you will get well."

She turned to Daniel and stared into his eyes with hope and desperation.

"Promise me, Daniel. Promise me that our beautiful girl will be alright."

There was a long silence—too long for Olivia, who had heard every word.

"Typical," said a voice deep inside her head. "He never was good at commitments."

Chapter Four

Olivia's coma had become a mélange of dreams, fantasies, extreme confusion, fear, joy, panic, eroticism, and genuine sensory perceptions that included smell, hearing, and touch. Much of what she was experiencing was repetitive. Most of it was Olivia talking to herself, deep in the recesses of her mind:

Am I dead?

What the hell happened?

If I am dead, why does my nose itch?

CAN SOMEONE SCRATCH MY NOSE, PLEASE?

Maybe this is Purgatory, like in Dante's "Divine Comedy."

But why would Purgatory smell like a hospital room?

No! This must be Hell. What other explanation can there be that infernal beeping of the heart monitor?

My God! How long have I been here?

I heard my mom and dad before, and Danny was here, too.

Olivia drifts off into a dreamlike state.

Oh, Danny!

God! Does he know how much I love him? Why is he so afraid of having a relationship with me? Look, there he is over by the nurses' station. I try to catch his eye but he doesn't see me. I continue toward the bank of elevators when suddenly I am pushed into the stairwell, my face is gently pressed against the wall. He presses me firmly against the cinder blocks, and from behind he pushes his body against me. I can feel how hard he is, and instantly my excitement is soaring. I can't believe I am already wet as he rhythmically rubs against me. He raises my skirt and caresses my thighs. Gently working his way up my legs and pulling down my panties, he loosens his grip on me and slowly works his hands around to my breasts. I am wearing no bra—I never do in my fantasies. I still have my back to him, but his breath on my neck and his fingers on my nipples are driving me crazy. He undoes his fly, and I can feel him. Suddenly, he lifts me up and carries me up a flight and to the landing where he lays me on my back. He removes the rest of my clothes, and his, and we are naked to the world, stripped of inhibitions, completely vulnerable—together. Rapturously, I anticipate his next move. He never fails me. Our conversation is sparse, deliberate, and ever so seductive. Soon he will enter me, and our bodies will begin to move as one. The momentum will build—incredibly—miraculously—and I will lose all control. I can feel it growing, blossoming, and accelerating throughout my body. Faster, faster, faster as he thrusts himself ever deeper into me, my soul, my entire being, I am thrilled beyond belief. And I know with absolute certainty, it is the same for him. At that very moment when we can hold back no longer, we climax together in a bellow of ecstasy—in unison—in unity—in a perfect moment of eternal union.

"Why me?" I whisper as I finally catch my breath. "Because there is no one but you, love," Daniel utters in a voice that seems divine. "Only you, Olivia . . . now and forever."

And then I sleep . . . a peaceful, perfect sleep.

The following morning, her breathing was normal, her oxygen levels were good so the decision was made to take Olivia off of the respirator—there was no medical reason not to endorse this course of action. And they could always put her back on it.

Olivia was completely aware of the removal of the breathing tube. She wanted to yell "OUCH," but she couldn't will her mouth to work. Her eyes also seemed to still be glued shut, and none of her muscles were responding.

With the god-awful beeping sound of the respirator finally gone, Olivia turned her attention to the hideous catheter inserted in her. Though it was certainly doing its job by eliminating the waste products from the liters of IV fluids they'd been pumping through her veins, her bladder felt like an over-inflated balloon about to burst.

Close to regaining consciousness, she listened attentively to the conversation between Daniel and a policeman named Eddie. They were talking about the growing investigation into Olivia's attempted murder—(*WHAT!*)—and what to expect in the coming days.

"We'll have to tell the Yard that Olivia's here in London—(*LONDON?*)—and once she comes to, they will want to interview her as soon as possible."

"I imagine they'll want to talk to me, as well," Daniel realized.

"You, Margaret, the security guards, everyone who was on the floor at the time of the attack, all of Olivia's known acquaintances from birth to the present, every email, Twitter, and Facebook posting she has ever made or received; pretty much every nook and cranny of her existence."

(WHAT!)

"Jesus! Does the police department have that kind of man-power?" Daniel asked Armstrong.

"You're talking about Scotland Bloody Yard, mate. We've got people in every broom closet from Chelsea to Birmingham."

Daniel sat deep in thought for a moment. Even Olivia could sense his distress. "Somehow, I have to think that a million MPS investigators working the case are not going to make her any safer," Daniel answered. "It's bound to get out where she is—how serious is this?"

"Very! Just like the I.R.A. used to do," the Inspector offered. "We just keep moving."

"Could someone please move me to the loo?" Olivia said out loud.

Olivia's parents were there in a matter of minutes. After a joyous, tearful reunion, replete with their daughter's glorious smile, Arthur Franklin collapsed into a chair and began bawling like a man who had just run over his daughter's kitten.

"Arthur, are you ok?" asked Daniel, who sensed that this was much more than tears of relief.

After a moment, Arthur removed his face from his cupped hands and gazed at Daniel through bleary, bloodshot eyes.

"I need to speak with you and Chief Inspector Armstrong," he muttered faintly. "Immediately!"

Elizabeth Franklin and her darling daughter Olivia were sharing a mother and daughter celebration of joy and gratitude that no man could possibly understand. Elizabeth could hardly believe that the near lifeless form she had sat beside the night before had been miraculously transformed into this beautiful, playful, bright-eyed beauty that she'd known all her life. Even her mother saw in Olivia something breathtakingly special. It wasn't just her physical beauty that was ever so striking; the personality and spirit of her daughter was selfless, giving, and compassionate. Olivia could look into the eyes of a dying child and soothe their pain and make them comfortable and even bring a smile. She had that effect on everyone.

As the party continued in Olivia's room, quite a different scenario was being played out in an empty lounge down the hall.

Arthur Franklin was pacing frantically, ranting, and pounding on tables and walls until his knuckles were bloody.

"It is all my fault," he kept shouting. "I am responsible for this. I did this."

Daniel Whittemore placed a comforting hand on Franklin's shoulder and tried to settle him down.

"Come sit down, Arthur. We're here to help you."

Daniel coaxed Arthur to a seat at the table, where the elderly physician proceeded to tell the most incredible story that either Whittemore or Armstrong had ever heard.

"I suppose you could say it all started in the 1970s," he began. "Elizabeth and I desperately wanted a family, but it just wasn't happening. This was more than a bit ironic, as I was the director of the Fertility Clinic at

Chelsea and Westminster Hospital at the time. I also had a private practice in Althorp, nearer to our home in Northampton. "

"For years, we tried everything, with no results—and for years, Elizabeth became so despondent that I became worried for her health. Her deepening depression became so severe that at one point she actually attempted suicide. Fortunately, I found her in the nick of time and pumped her stomach of every last pill we had in the house. It was about that time that my own depression took hold and my judgment became clouded. NO! NOT CLOUDED! CRIMINAL!" he shouted.

Armstrong and Whittemore looked at each other in total bewilderment. It was the policeman who spoke first.

"Dr. Franklin, I have one question for you . . . did you try to kill your daughter?"

"WHAT?" Franklin shouted.

"Good," said Chief Inspector Armstrong, putting his feet up on the desk. "Now, let's get on with it."

Olivia's father seemed to settle down and continued with his story.

He told them that on December 24th, 1980, a sweet and innocent-looking young woman named Mary Wagner walked into his office. She had an appointment to have her eggs harvested and fertilized. Her chauffeur, Phillip, came in with her and did most of the talking. He said that he was carrying the semen for the fertilization. Mary Wagner, clearly emotional over this, tearfully explained to him that her fiancé wanted her eggs harvested and fertilized with his semen to guarantee that she was fertile and probably could conceive a child. There would be no marriage without proof of fertility. This was both extremely unusual and very distasteful to Dr. Franklin. The point was that if she were unable to conceive, the family of her fiancé would not allow the marriage to go forth. Furthermore, Dr. Franklin would have to guarantee that she would remain a virgin and that her hymen would be intact. That part wasn't an issue since the surgery was done using a laparoscope through the abdomen.

Mary Wagner's chauffeur, Phillip, then explained to Dr. Franklin that the eggs were to be fertilized and, after proven viable, they were to be destroyed. Dr. Franklin agreed to the terms and the procedure was scheduled for the following morning, Christmas Day.

The procedure went off without a hitch. Doctor Franklin was given Phillip's phone number to call the moment the fertilization was confirmed and that, he thought, was that.

Chief Inspector Armstrong shifted in his seat.

"Well, I can't say I see any crime here," he offered. "And I certainly can't imagine how this makes you responsible for that or for Olivia's attack."

Dr. Franklin took a moment to wipe the tears from his eyes, and blow his nose into a handkerchief.

"There's just a little bit more," he said in a cracking voice.

"Later that morning, I called Elizabeth and asked her to come to my office. I told her I had some startling news that just couldn't wait and assured her that she would be absolutely thrilled."

"When my wife arrived a short time later, I explained that I'd been visited that morning by a lovely young couple from a well-to-do family who wanted to make an extraordinary contribution to a worthy patient of my choosing. She and her husband already had three beautiful children of their own and they wanted to donate one of their viable embryos for implantation in a woman less fortunate. Five days later, I did just that, implanting the viable stolen embryo into my wife."

"It happens that quickly?" asked the Inspector.

"Actually, fertilization is instantaneous," the doctor explained. "The moment a sperm comes in contact with an egg, the zygote is formed. We use the term 'viable zygote,' which is really a misnomer, only after mitosis or cell division begins. After five days, there has been sufficient cell division to proceed with implantation. The embryo was ready."

"So what?" said Daniel, seeming a tad puzzled.

"I'm afraid I don't get it either," said Armstrong. "You didn't tell this Wagner lady that one of the zygotes/embryos wasn't destroyed. Okay, so that's rather unethical, but I rather doubt it's a crime."

"Actually it is, Inspector. When I called the chauffeur Phillip, I told him that the zygotes were all viable and that they all had been destroyed, that was, in fact, a crime."

"Oh, come on, Arthur. It's not like you stole the crown jewels. What's the big deal?" said Daniel.

"Interesting choice of words, Doctor." Franklin came back. "You see, the 'big deal,' as you call it, occurred the following February, when Mary Wagner was suddenly all over the news. She was absolutely radiant, just as I remembered her—truly breathtaking as she stood at the side of her betrothed—the Prince of Wales."

Chapter Five

Later that night, after everyone had left except for Daniel Whittemore and Eddie Armstrong, the two of them sat in the hospital cafeteria, brainstorming the *whos, whats, whens, whys* and *hows* of this most bizarre case.

"OK, let's go over it again," said Armstrong, tearing out the pages of flow charts and diagrams he'd been working on for the last hour. He set them aside neatly in front of him so he could reference them as he constructed his next crude diagram of times, places, people, events, and possible motives.

"I think mine has more arrows, circles and boxes," said his weary friend, Danny, pointing to his own scribbling.

"Yes, but mine has more question marks, which is what we are looking for," said the detective.

"Excuse me! I thought we were looking for answers."

"Well, we can't very well find the answers if we don't know the questions," he answered with a sly grin.

"Right!" said the doctor.

"Okay, let's try it a little differently this time," said the Chief Inspector. "Make a list titled *Who*. By *Who*, I mean every single person you have come in contact with since the orderly yelled 'code blue' and any other names you can think of who might be associated with this. Try to be precise. Leave no one out, right up to this moment."

"What are you going to do?" Daniel asked.

"I'm going to get us some coffee," said Eddie, rising from his chair.

"So, what have you got?" Eddie asked Daniel a short time later. "Have you solved the case?"

"Well, best as I can recall, it began with the orderly, whose name I do not know, yelling 'code blue.' I guess that makes him a suspect, right?"

"Actually, at the present time, there are just under seven billion suspects residing on this planet of ours. The purpose of this exercise is to try and narrow that list a bit."

"Right!" Daniel answered. "Moving right along, the next person I saw after the orderly were several dozen doctors and nurses I blew past, none of whom I can name."

"The Yard is already working on that, if they haven't already completed that list."

"Okay, so I ran into the room where Olivia was—there were already two nurses doing CPR, and a moment later, my chief pediatric intensivist nurse practitioner, Margaret, entered the room. Next came a few more nurses with a crash cart—I assume your blokes at the MPS already know their names; then two orderlies with a gurney came in to move Olivia down to the ER.

"I presume that, mixed in with all those people, however briefly it may have been, was Olivia's attacker," Daniel added.

"Very good," Chief Inspector Armstrong noted. "We may make a detective out of you yet."

"So let me ask you," Armstrong continued, "What was the attacker wearing?"

"Nah, nah, nah. You're not going to snare me with that one. The attacker could have been wearing anything from a bikini to a space suit, though it's reasonable to assume that he was probably dressed in hospital garb."

"He?" said Eddie, noticeably disappointed.

"I mean He, She, or both," Daniel answered.

"Both?" said Armstrong. "Now you've got me confused."

"Well, who's to say that it was just a man or a woman? Isn't it possible that a pair of perpetrators could have snuck into that room, waited for just the right moment, then pounced on the shoulder of the unsuspecting victim, thrusting the hypo into Olivia's neck? They probably did not have medical training."

"Well, that would explain why he missed the carotid," Armstrong said sarcastically.

"Okay. I get your point. Now, let's get back to your list. Who else is on there?"

"We got to the ER, where there were five or six nurses and doctors, including Dr. Falkner, the cardiologist; Dr. Blythe, the pulmonologist; Dobbs, who's the head of Emergency Services; Margaret Osborne, who came down with me; and the ER resident, John Wolsey, who told us about the telltale trickle of blood on Olivia's neck. Oh, and by the way, this coffee sucks."

"Just keep going, Danny, you're doing great."

"Well, after that, there was John Parker and Guy Devon, the security guards who helped me and Margaret steal the ambulance—and thank you for taking care of that, by the way—and the next people we saw were you and Donnie at the London Clinic. Then you called your friend, Nigel something-or-other to supervise the investigation at Radcliffe and buy us some time, and that's about it."

"No, wait. There was also the taxi driver who took me to fetch the Franklins by way of the Acropolis and Disneyworld," Whittemore added. "So, how'd I do?" Daniel asked his friend.

"Very impressive!" he answered. "You only left out two key figures."

"Really? Who's that?"

"Mary Wagner and Phillip, her driver."

Danny and Eddie went round and round for quite a while, still trying to sort out the *whos, whats, whens, whys* and *hows* of the whole affair. They had a thousand questions that they couldn't get a handle on, but then, in an instant, they had a breakthrough.

Eddie scratched a question on his pad and held it up for Daniel to see. The words read:

WHY NOW?

They finally decided that another interview was in order with Arthur Franklin, the only person they could think of who might shed some light on that question. They placed a call to the Franklin's home and announced that they were coming over.

After hemming and hawing about the lateness of the hour, Franklin finally acceded to their demand on one condition:

"I'll tell you whatever you want to know, but only if Elizabeth is left out of the conversation. She doesn't know anything anyway."

They agreed to his stipulation (if only for the time being) and headed to Knightsbridge.

Outside the home of Arthur and Elizabeth Franklin, a black Mini Cooper was parked just down the road with a good view of the Franklin's front door. The car contained just one individual who had followed the Franklins both to and from The London Clinic. Sitting there patiently, preparing the device, he had already scoped out the best location to place it for maximum effect.

"Bugger!" he shouted, pounding the dashboard as a car pulled up to the front of the residence and two men he didn't recognize went quickly inside. He'd been frustrated for the past few days by one thing after another. First off, the girl hadn't died. Second, they had snuck her off to an unknown location that he hadn't been able to track down because the Franklins kept taking taxis from the Wild Goose Chase Cab Company. That was, until this morning, when they dashed out of the house, jumped into their Jaguar, and sped off to the London Clinic.

By the time he reached the lobby of The London Clinic, the Franklins were nowhere to be seen. A check of the hospital registry showed no Olivia Franklin—checked in under an alias, no doubt. (Incidentally, nurse Margaret Osborne, who, with a few taps on a notebook computer while in the back of the ambulance, alerted the Clinic that a VIP was on route and they had to admit her under the name Melissa Nicholls.)

"Bloody hell," the man said to no one as he sat in his car, plotting his next move.

Inside Arthur Franklin's library, the three men sat comfortably in over-stuffed leather chairs. Whiskey and cigars were optional.

Chief Inspector Armstrong began the conversation.

"Arthur . . . may I call you Arthur?"

"You might as well. You're drinking my whiskey."

"Listen," Armstrong continued. "Daniel and I have been all over this for hours. There's just one thing that's got us so confused."

"And what's that, Detective?"

"Why now?" Armstrong answered.

"I think I'll have a whiskey, as well," Franklin remarked, moving to a nearby chair.

The three of them sat there just staring at one another. Then Arthur Franklin spoke. "It began about three weeks ago—February 11th or thereabouts. There was a fundraiser for the Childhood Cancer Research Group at Oxford Radcliffe. The evening was positively lovely, especially for my wife and me. Everyone in the room seemed to adore Olivia. People kept coming over to us to rave about our 'brilliant daughter,' our 'amazingly gifted daughter,' 'what a special person she is.' There were children there, too, and they followed her around like she was a famous movie star. Olivia was stunning. 'Look at her,' Elizabeth said to me. 'She's the belle of the ball.' 'Indeed, she is,' I commented. 'Our gift from god has grown into a most remarkable woman.'"

Franklin took a sip of whiskey and continued with his story.

"As the evening was wrapping up, after too many hours of cocktails and hors d'oeuvres, I noticed Olivia was talking to someone at the opposite end of the room. She looked very animated, as is her way. Her head was thrown back as she laughed, and her gestures were broad but elegant."

"From the back, the man looked very distinguished. He was wearing a dress uniform and appeared to be someone important. "

"As Elizabeth and I walked over, both Olivia and the gentleman she was speaking with turned toward us. I'm afraid my shock was immediate, though I tried my best to hide it. I was face to face with a man I hadn't seen in 30 years.

"Olivia introduced him to her mother and me. I could barely raise my arm to shake his hand. I knew that I didn't look the same—neither did he. I knew him nonetheless. 'Mom, Dad, I would like you to meet Lt. Colonel Phillip Churchill. Lt. Colonel Churchill has been a significant contributor to the Center for some years, and I am so glad that I finally have the opportunity to meet him and thank him for his support.'

"I wasn't sure if Churchill recognized me or my name," Arthur went on, "but I didn't know if Olivia had discussed us before we joined them. Lt. Colonel Churchill seemed quite infatuated with Olivia and barely seemed to notice that Elizabeth and I were standing there. But, from the moment I saw Churchill standing with Olivia, I had this dire premonition. I can't explain it. I just knew."

Phillip Churchill sat behind the wheel of his Mini Cooper, waiting for the departure of Franklin's visitors. Even as they said their goodbyes beneath the light above the doorway, he didn't recognize them. They looked like a couple of businessmen, plain and simple.

After shaking hands with Dr. Franklin, they walked to a nearby Land Rover and began to drive away. They had barely started to roll away from the Franklin's residence when their car was suddenly rocked as if snatched by a giant earthquake.

In his rearview mirror, Daniel saw a gigantic fireball lighting up the night sky. They looked at each other in horror.

Driving off in the night, puffing on his cigar, Churchill smiled and congratulated himself on such a spectacular explosion. He leaned forward and turned up the volume on Andrea Bocelli's "Time To Say Goodbye" and sang along.

Chapter Six

At Armstrong's direction, they did not turn around to investigate the explosion.

"We just can't risk it," he explained. "Whoever did this may have seen us, and one time is one too many. Besides, we have to get to Olivia as quickly as possible. And now, if you'll excuse me, I have a couple of calls to make."

The first call Eddie made was to his friend Nigel Prescott, who had been supervising the "Missing Person" investigation at Oxford Radcliffe.

"Nigel, it's Eddie Armstrong . . . yes, I know what time it is, and I'm sorry, but it's something of an emergency . . . I have reason to believe that there is going to be another attempt on Olivia Franklin's life, if it hasn't already happened . . . I need you to send some men over to London Acute, room 1035 . . . yes . . . outside the room, down at the entrance and especially at the information desk at the entrance . . . we're looking for a man by the name of Phillip Churchill."

"Phillip Churchill?" said Prescott. "The Chief of Royal Security?"

"Ah, shit!" said Armstrong. "Meet me at the clinic straight away."

Prescott met Armstrong and Whittemore at the Acute Care Clinic. After checking on Olivia, who was fast asleep in her bed, they gathered in the lounge down the hall.

"What the bloody hell is going on here, Eddie?" Prescott asked. "First, you've got me playing this charade at Radcliffe, looking for a woman you already had; then I find out that her parents were killed by some bloke who blew up their house and half of Knightsbridge; and now you're telling me that the top man in the Queen's Royal Guard may be behind all this?"

"That's pretty much it," said Armstrong.

Prescott was almost speechless. He was having great difficulty getting his head around what Armstrong was telling him. He was numb.

"Now what?" was all Prescott could say.

"Okay, here's my thinking," Eddie speculated. "Churchill probably followed the Franklins to the clinic when they got word she'd awakened from her coma. We were so excited that nobody thought to remind them of the need to take precautions so they wouldn't be followed. So, Churchill knows Olivia's here. Because of the alias she's using, he may not have found out what room she's in. Even if he has that information, he hasn't formulated his plan to try and take her out again. That gives us a slight edge."

"How much of an edge?" Dr. Whittemore asked.

"Well, for practical purposes, let's assume it's narrower than a straight razor."

"So, how do you want to proceed?" asked Prescott.

"Danny, I need you to go home and get some rest. Tomorrow morning, I want you to pack a small travel bag, just the essentials, as if you were going away for a three-day holiday, and be at the Hertz car hire at Marble Arch at noon. Drive your own car there."

"Nigel, I need you to keep Olivia safe until she leaves the hospital between 11:00 a.m. and noon tomorrow to meet Danny at Hertz."

"And how's that going to work?" Prescott asked.

"I don't have it all worked out yet, but I will by morning. I'll be here for the rest of the night, making arrangements and writing up the details of my plan so we're all on the same page, so to speak. The important thing is that we've got to make Olivia disappear before Churchill can get to her."

"Armstrong," Prescott began. "I'll go along with this until Olivia has left the hospital. But the moment she's away, you and I are going to have a serious sit-down. I'm already pretty deep into I-don't-know-what. But tomorrow, you're going to tell me every last detail of what this is all about. You follow?"

"I swear, Nigel. Right down to the shitty coffee they serve in the café."

At roughly the same time that Danny, Eddie, and Nigel were meeting at the hospital, Phillip Churchill and several of his deputies were meeting in his office in Buckingham Palace.

"So, here's what we've got so far," Churchill explained. "On March 5th, we received a tip from one of our informants at Sinn Fein that a radical cell calling themselves 'The Real Brotherhood' was planning an attack on the upcoming wedding between Prince William and Kate Middleton. We have no details whatsoever about the nature of the plot, other than the fact that a key member of this cell is a physician by the name of Olivia Franklin who works at Oxford Radcliffe Hospital. We don't have a picture, but she's been described as being extremely attractive, roughly 5'10" tall, 130 lbs., long blond hair, usually worn down, black, horn-rimmed spectacles. "

"Anyway, I went to Radcliffe later that day, only to discover that Franklin was being treated in the Emergency Room for some kind of injury she'd sustained that morning; by the time I got clearance from medical staff to see her, she had disappeared."

"Disappeared?" said Major Richard Ripley. "What does that mean?"

"Gone, missing, whereabouts unknown," said Churchill. "By 11:00 that night, the hospital was crawling with police trying to find Olivia Franklin."

"Sounds like she was tipped off," said another major.

"Apparently so," said Churchill.

"So, what's the big deal?" said Major Ryan Wright. "A bunch of IRA maniacs, some of them double-agents, as usual, are tripping all over one another feeding us information, and feeding it right back to Franklin. This doesn't sound like much of a problem to me. With a breakdown

35

like that, Olivia Franklin is clearly out of business and probably on her way to never-be-seen-again-land."

"One would think so," said Churchill. "Except for the fact that I got word this morning that she's still in London, at the London Acute Care, which makes me wonder if she's still planning to go ahead with whatever this is. As such, we will all be going there first thing in the morning in plainclothes to see if we can find her."

At approximately 10:30 the next morning, an elderly couple, both in their seventies, was observed by one of Churchill's men as they entered the hospital. He paid them little notice, though he did hear them say something about the difficult rehab "Melissa" was facing for her shattered femur. About an hour later, as the rest of Churchill's people were going room to room looking for Olivia, that same elderly couple exited the hospital, along with a nurse pushing a wheelchair that held a dark-haired woman with a scarf around her neck that partially obscured her face, and an elevated left leg in a hip to ankle plaster cast.

"Good luck, Melissa," the nurse was heard to say as she helped her patient into Edward Armstrong's parents' car.

Inside the vehicle on their way to the Hertz Rental Agency at Marble Arch, Olivia removed the dummy cast from her leg, discarded the scarf and black wig she'd been wearing, and put a trench coat on over her clothes from the travel bag the Armstrongs had brought her, which also contained her passport. She then expressed her profound gratitude to her rescuers.

After circling the parking lot a couple of times, Olivia exited the car at the Hertz office precisely at noon. A moment later, she was in the arms of Daniel Whittemore.

Their embrace, which clearly reflected their huge sense of relief and growing optimism, was much longer and closer than merely a joyous greeting between friends.

"I've waited a long time for this," Olivia finally said.

"Me too," said Daniel, gazing lovingly into her amazing blue eyes.

Five minutes later, using her American Express card, Olivia rented a car from Hertz for a period of two weeks.

"Now what?" she asked Daniel.

"Where do you keep most of your money?" he asked her.

"Barclays on Churchill Street," she answered.

"Excellent. That's my bank, too. Okay here's the deal. There's a parking structure on Canary Row that's just a short walk to Barclays. That's our first stop. I'll tell you the rest of Chief Inspector Armstrong's plan on the way."

"Let's do it."

Chapter Seven

Olivia and Danny parked the car in a covered garage on Canary Row, and walked from there to Barclays. There was much to do.

First, they closed all of their accounts, with the exception of their Barclaycards. Next, they exchanged most of their British pounds to Euros, bought several prepaid debit cards that could be used anywhere, converted some of their funds to other currencies, including Swiss francs, deutschmarks, and U.S. dollars, and wired some funds to an account that Daniel had at HSBC, which had branches all over Europe, Russia, and the Middle East. In all, they were carrying or had otherwise stashed nearly half a million pounds.

Next, they exited One Churchill Street and hailed a cab to take them to 235 Regent Street.

"What about the rental car?" Olivia asked.

"We're done with that," Daniel answered. "If they are trying to track you, the trail ends there."

"Not that I mind the intrigue—it's kind of cool, actually—but what's this all about?" Olivia asked him.

"Olivia, I have a great deal to tell you, a lot of it pretty dreadful, but you'll have to wait just a little bit longer. We have too much to do before we catch the ferry. I promise I'll tell you everything on the way to France."

"France," said Olivia without a trace of emotion. "France," she said again in the same, empty tone.

Nothing more was said until they arrived at the Apple store on Regent Street to make one young salesman the happiest man in England.

About an hour later, they walked out of Apple with two fully loaded wireless laptop computers, two iPhones with all the bells and whistles, and two iPads. They added many apps including comprehensive travel guides. All of it was paid for in cash. One more stop was the nearby AT&T store to pick up several pre-paid international cell phones.

After hailing a taxi—destination, Gatwick Airport—Daniel worked on his laptop while giving Olivia instructions for things to be doing on hers. They conducted their conversation in whispers so that the driver would not overhear them.

"Okay, fire away," Olivia said.

"First you need to go to Yahoo and open a new email account. No user name or password that you've ever used before."

"Right," she answered and began tapping away.

After a few minutes Olivia said, "Okay, just check this before I hit Enter. The account belongs to John Williams, age 16, of New York City."

"Nice," said Danny. "Go on."

"His username is bigboy1637—password: statueofliberty—security question1: Where did you spend your honeymoon?—answer: To be determined—security question 2: What is the name of the street on which you grew up?—answer: Broadway—no alternative email address given."

"Fantastic," said Danny. "Couldn't be better."

"Now, go to the American Airlines website and check flights and availability from Gatwick to New York's JFK."

"I'm on it," Olivia responded. She was there faster than Newton's apple fell from the tree.

"Okay, the next available flight is at 8:00 tonight."

Danny looked at his watch and saw that it was 4:50 p.m.

"Perfect," he answered. "Make a first-class reservation under your real name and use the same card you used for the rental car."

"Won't that put them back on our trail?" Olivia asked.

"Yes," said Daniel, glancing at his watch. "And right on schedule."

While Olivia was dealing with American Airlines, Danny purchased two tickets in their real names for the EuroStar Chunnel train from St. Pancras Station to Gare du Nord in Paris, leaving at 9:00 p.m. He used his Barclaycard.

"All set," said Olivia. "Flight 107, scheduled to leave on time …Daniel, I need to call my parents and tell them what's going on."

Daniel hesitated a moment before answering.

"We'll deal with all of that on the ferry," he answered.

A few minutes later . . . "Sir, we are approaching the airport. Which airline are you flying?"

"American Airlines," Daniel told him. Then, turning to Olivia, "Care for a holiday?" he said with a smile.

"Where to?" she asked sweetly.

"I only wish I knew," he answered cryptically.

Inspectors Armstrong and Prescott were walking the halls of the London Acute Care, looking for anything that might set off their antennas.

"So, how is it you know of Churchill?" Armstrong asked his colleague.

"We worked together back in '81 on the wedding of Charles and Diana. I think the bigger question is, why don't you know of him?"

"That would be because I spent most of '80 and'81 in Sydney working with the Australian Federal Police on a training program we developed on investigative practices," Armstrong explained. "Do you know him personally, Nigel?"

"We met a couple of times during security planning. Those buggers in Northern Ireland were a real worry back then. That said, the Metropolitan Police has never worked closely with the Royal Guard. They're all military and don't much care for sharing information with us lowly cops."

"Military, huh? Well, that explains a couple of things."

"Such as?" Prescott queried.

"Well, for one thing, they aren't worth their salt, so far as detective work is concerned. Otherwise, Churchill would have known Olivia was at London Acute Care in the blink of an eye."

"And two?" Prescott asked.

"He had no qualms about blowing up half of Knightsbridge to eliminate the Franklins."

"Blimey!" exclaimed Prescott, not at all responding to what Armstrong had just said. "There he is—coming right toward us. What do we do?"

"Just play dumb for the moment. Let's see what happens."

"Prescott isn't it . . . Scotland Yard?" asked Churchill, quite calm and relaxed.

"Yes, Sir," Prescott answered. "I'm surprised you remember me, Sir."

"Never forget a face," he said, extending his hand and giving Armstrong the once-over.

"So, what brings you here?" Churchill asked him while continuing to stare at Armstrong, who quickly jumped in.

"My partner and I are looking for a woman who mysteriously disappeared from Oxford Radcliffe a couple of days ago."

"Pardon my manners, Lt. Colonel Churchill. This is Chief Inspector Edward Armstrong. We're working the case together."

"Pleasure to meet you, Armstrong. And a strange coincidence this is, indeed."

"How's that?" asked Armstrong.

"We, too, are looking for a woman who disappeared from Radcliffe. Perhaps we can compare notes on this," Churchill suggested.

"Brilliant!" Prescott replied. "There's a lounge right down the hall we can use."

"Ah, let me round up my team and we'll meet you there in 30 minutes. Say, 5:30 p.m. or so?"

"Excellent," said Armstrong, seeking to take advantage of this rare opportunity.

As Churchill was turning to leave, Prescott asked him one more question.

"Excuse me, Sir. Why is the Royal Guard working a missing person's case?"

Churchill continued toward the door. "I'm afraid that's classified for the moment," he said as he left the room.

"I could have written that line myself," said Armstrong.

Standing outside the American Airlines terminal at Gatwick Airport, Daniel quietly went over the plan one last time. Then he made a phone call to Eddie Armstrong, praying to get the green light to take this critical next step.

"We're at the airport," he said without as much as a hello. "Do we have any reason to think that Churchill has put out a broader net?"

"No," he said unequivocally. "It's even better than that, my friend. Churchill's here at Acute Care. I just shook his hand and I have a meeting with him in five minutes. We're going to work together as a not-so-joint task-force which, in the spirit of Queen and country, will inform him shortly that Olivia has been using her credit card this afternoon."

"So we're right on schedule," Danny said.

"Yes we are, and for the moment, we've got the upper hand. Call me on my cell when you get to the beach," he added before ending the call.

A moment later, Daniel and Olivia made a big show of affection with hugs and kisses and a tearful 'Bon Voyage.' The kisses were the only part of the scene that required no acting. A rush of memories filled Olivia's head. She knew she had to focus.

Seconds after that, Olivia and her two carry-on bags—one with clothing and personal items, the other with her computers and such—disappeared into the terminal.

Daniel lingered a moment, got back into the still-waiting taxi, and made a somewhat unusual request.

"I'll give you 50 quid if you'll drive me around for twenty minutes and then drop me at the American Airlines Baggage Claim."

"Very well," said the driver enthusiastically.

Inside the airport, Olivia picked up her boarding pass at an electronic kiosk and moved quickly through security, where her bags were searched and her passport was efficiently scanned.

Fifteen minutes later, after strolling along the concourse without incident, she exited the terminal through the AA Baggage Claim doors, where a familiar-looking taxi and a very distinguished gentleman were waiting at the curb.

"Pleasant trip?" Daniel asked her with a sly smile.

They entered the taxi and held each other closely.

Inside the room where Armstrong and Prescott were to meet in a matter of minutes with Churchill and his men, the two policemen went over a few quick items.

"Here's my thinking," said Armstrong to Prescott. "This started as a lone wolf operation, but after Churchill blew his initial attempt and then lost Olivia, he brought in some of his closest deputies, who probably know next to nothing about what's really going on. Anyway, he now sees us as a possible resource to help him track down Olivia."

"So, we see how he plays it, keeping our cards close to the vest," suggested Prescott.

"Precisely," Armstrong answered. "We tell them as little as possible, and learn as much as we can, before charging Churchill with the crimes."

"Got it!" Prescott answered.

"Ah, Gentlemen," said Churchill as he entered the room with three other men. He introduced them to Armstrong and Prescott as "members of his team"—Richard Ripley, James Townsend, and Ryan Wright.

"So, Prescott, what have you got?" Churchill asked, taking the lead.

"On the 5th of March, a Dr. Olivia Franklin, who works at John Radcliffe Hospital, was attacked by someone using a hypodermic needle, apparently intent on killing her."

Armstrong was carefully watching the faces of the other majors to gauge their reactions. They weren't giving much away.

"Any suspects?" asked Churchill.

"Not a one," said Prescott. "Anyway," he continued, "shortly after being revived in the ER, Dr. Franklin managed to slip out of the building and went completely missing for two days. As she was still in pretty bad condition when she left, we began by checking other hospitals."

"I assume you all have these," Armstrong interjected, pulling out several copies of Olivia's Hospital I.D. photo, which he gave to each of the Royal Guardsman.

No one said a word, and their blank expressions were more than a little telling.

"Anyway, we were able to use these photos to track Franklin to London Acute Care, but by the time we got there, she was gone again."

At that moment, Edward Armstrong reached into his pocket and hit the send key, which was set on speed dial. Then he ended the call. Ten seconds later his phone rang, and he pushed away from the table to take the call. A few seconds after that, he interrupted the men at the table with important news.

"There's been activity on Olivia's credit card this afternoon. She rented a car at the Hertz at Marble Arch and bought an American Airlines ticket for a flight from Gatwick to New York at 8:00 this evening."

Everyone glanced at their watches in unison—it was just after six.

"Let's move," said Churchill, and they all ran for the door.

There could not have been a soul at Gatwick that wasn't wondering what was going on.

Despite the constant reassurance of the police that everything was fine, the sheer numbers of security forces running about the airport was cause for alarm.

Having confirmed that Olivia Franklin had passed through security, Churchill and his men were off to Gate 20, while everyone else was checking every bar, restaurant, newsstand, restroom, and maintenance closet for anyone who might fit Olivia's description. Tall women with other hair colors were checked for wigs, despite the fact that the video at the security station showed her as a blonde with shoulder length hair, probably because she needed to look like her passport.

Finally, Armstrong and Prescott walked to the gate where they encountered Phillip Churchill, who kept looking at his watch.

"Do you think she could have had an accomplice to get her from Radcliffe to London Acute?" Churchill asked Prescott.

"I think it's rather likely," Prescott answered. "But no one we've identified, as of yet."

"Hmm," said Churchill, his mind racing through myriad possibilities. "Do you know who Dr. Daniel Whittemore is?" he finally asked.

"He's on my list of people to interview," Armstrong quickly answered. "Why?"

"When I was over at Radcliffe this afternoon, I overheard someone casually remark that they hadn't seen him in a few days, some kind of family emergency. Coincidence?"

Armstrong quickly pulled out his cell phone and hit a number on his speed dial.

"Smitty? It's Armstrong. Can you do your magic computer stuff and tell me if there has been any credit card activity today by a Dr. Daniel Whittemore? Yes, I'll hold."

As the hands on Churchill's watch were racing towards 8:00 p.m., he was visibly agitated, which Armstrong certainly noticed. Finally:

"Thanks Smitty, you're a gem."

"What?" said Churchill, whose frustration was obvious.

"Dr. Daniel Whittemore's Barclaycard was used about three hours ago to book two tickets on the 9:00 p.m. Chunnel train to from St. Pancras Station to Gare du Nord in Paris."

"Bloody EuroStar!" said Armstrong.

Armstrong was on his walkie in less than a second.

"Prescott . . . come back!"

"What is it, Eddie?" Prescott answered.

"It looks like we may have been snookered," said Armstrong. "Here's what we need to do. I need men at the gate and I need someone to check with every other airline to see if she may have changed her ticket. I also need you to dispatch units to the Chunnel embarkation point at St. Pancras. Call me on my cell if anything turns up here."

"The Chunnel?" said Prescott, sounding very surprised.

"Yes," Armstrong answered. "It looks like that Whittemore guy is trying to get her to Paris."

"I'm on it, Eddie. Stay in touch."

"Let's move it," said Armstrong to Churchill. "There's still enough time to grab them."

Chapter Eight

On the ferry from Dover to Calais, Daniel and Olivia sat on the upper deck, huddled beneath a blanket.

"There's something I have to tell you, sweetheart," Whittemore said softly. He'd been using that term all day in his mind now he said it out loud, and Olivia really liked it.

"Is this a good something or a bad something?" she asked.

"I'm afraid it's both," he answered quietly.

After a moment's pause, Olivia said, "Let's start with the good something, okay?"

Daniel turned to face her so he could look into her eyes.

"For a long time now I have anguished over how we broke up. I didn't think that I was ready for a serious relationship and I didn't want to hurt you," he began. "I suspect you know this, what you don't know is that the struggle I have fought was because I never thought that a professor should get involved with a student." He paused for a moment, to find the right words. "Before I knew it, we were no longer professor and student but colleagues and no longer together. Olivia, I have never gotten over you. I know now just how important you are to me and when you were in a coma I vowed that when you were ready I would tell you just how I felt about you and just how wrong I was. Well, the thing is," he began, " you mean the world to me . . . you are my . . . my everything."

Before he could continue, Olivia broke in.

"Dr. Whittemore," she said in a tone that was all too serious. "I think it's fair to say that, under the circumstances." She said with a smile, and then she kissed Daniel "You may continue now.

"To put it another way," he continued, "Olivia Franklin, I'm in love with you."

It didn't take a moment for Olivia to throw her arms around Daniel and begin sobbing.

A few moments later, Daniel said, "Is that good crying, or bad crying?"

"Oh, shut up," she answered. Then, a few seconds after that . . . "I mean, shut up, my love."

Following several minutes of hugging and kissing and crying and laughing, Olivia announced that she was famished, and they moved to the Club Lounge. It was only a 90-minute cruise on the Pride of Canterbury from Dover to Calais, and they had left Mother England at 8:00 p.m. It was already 8:45 p.m., so there wasn't really time for a full meal, just a snack.

"So, when are you going to tell me all the bad things?" Olivia asked as they munched on their sandwiches.

Daniel looked into her eyes and let out a deep sigh.

"And, is it safe to call my parents now?" she added.

"I...I don't think we should do that on the boat. The hotel would be better."

"And which hotel is that?" Olivia asked him.

"I don't know about you," Daniel answered, "but I am completely wiped out."

"I concur completely. I am ragged. So what's the plan?" Olivia asked.

"There's a small hotel in Calais, not five minutes from the dock—I thought we'd hole up there for a while. It's little known, has 24-hour room service, and the one time I stayed there, they let me pay in cash. What do you think?" Daniel asked her.

"I think breakfast, lunch, and dinner in bed sounds simply grand."

By the time Daniel and Olivia checked into the Hotel Meurice, putting down a sizable cash deposit above and beyond the room rate, the hounds in London had lost the scent of their quarry, leaving them both frustrated and clueless.

It was Prescott who suggested that they pick things up in the morning.

"Can we meet at Scotland Yard?" he asked Churchill.

Appearing somewhat reluctant, Churchill agreed to be there with his team at 10:00 a.m.

"Well, that went pretty well, don't you think?" Prescott asked Armstrong, who couldn't help but smile.

"Nothing like an old fashioned game of hare and hounds to perk up your day," Armstrong said.

"Can you be at the office by 8:00 a.m.?" Armstrong asked as he headed for the Tube that would take him back to his flat.

"We have much to discuss," Prescott noted.

The first thing Daniel and Olivia did when they got to their room was strip off their clothes and jump into bed. It was no slow, lingering affair with gentle stroking and long deep kisses. This was more of a matter of urgency for both of them—making up for lost years.

"I thought I'd order some drinks and dinner," Daniel suggested after getting out of bed and putting on a robe. "Any preferences?"

"Are we going to have that talk?" Olivia asked.

"I think we'd better," Daniel answered.

"Select something scrumptious for dinner—you choose. And get me a bottle of Bombay gin and a bucket of ice," she added with a smile. "I'm going to take a shower."

While Olivia was in the shower, Daniel made a call. Armstrong was just getting home and surmised whom it was.

"Hi. It's me," said Daniel.

"Go on," said the detective.

"We decided to stay at the beach tonight. It's been a pretty hectic day."

"I'll say. Everything OK?"

"Pretty much. I haven't told her everything, yet. I'll be doing that shortly over dinner."

"Got a pencil and something to write on?" Armstrong asked.

"One sec . . . okay, go."

"In lower case letters, one word, write noshitsherlock@gmail.com. It's a new account just activated today. Using your new computer, send me your email address. I will have a report for you, probably by noon tomorrow. Sleep well, my friend." The line went dead.

The dinner Daniel arranged was anything but extravagant. When he called room service, he'd asked to speak to the chef. Marcel, it turned out, was quite amiable, and when Daniel told him this was for a very special young woman who has had several horrible days, Marcel said, "Do not even order, Monsieur. I will take care of everything."

"That's wonderful, Marcel, but please include a bottle of Bombay gin for the lady."

"Consider it done. And now if you please, I must excuse myself. I have a special meal to prepare."

The waiter came into the room with the table adorned with a linen cloth, fresh-cut flowers, candles, a beautiful bowl of mixed green salad with tomatoes and French dressing and two silver-covered dishes. On the table there was also an assortment of desserts, cheeses, and fruits. It was hard not to be impressed.

After generously tipping the waiter Daniel fixed Olivia a Bombay gin martini. As he poured himself a single malt scotch, Olivia couldn't help peeking under one of the silver covered dishes to reveal a plate of coq au vin; French comfort food. It smelled delicious; she couldn't wait to dig in.

"Before we begin to indulge in this amazing feast, I have to call my parents. I am sure that Eddie has been keeping them in the loop but I also know that they would rest easier hearing my voice and I would fell better hearing theirs."

Daniel quickly told her that they should eat now and call them after dinner. Their food might get too cold and she needed to keep her strength up. His eyes filled up but Olivia didn't see; she was marveling at the food in front of her.

"This should hold me for a while," Olivia said as she approached Daniel confidently and gave him a kiss.

"It's rather nice out tonight," he commented. "Shall we take our drinks out on the balcony?"

"Let's."

While Daniel was thrilled on so many levels—his indescribable elation over the miracle of Olivia, the love of his life, his dream come true—he was also scared, confused, and horrified by the thought of telling Olivia about her parents. After a while, she seemed to notice.

"Listen, love . . . why don't we try to eat, and you can give me the bad news after dinner and before dessert. Whatever it is, we'll handle it together."

Daniel appeared stoic, but Olivia knew that something bad was coming. The two of them just held each other for nearly two minutes. Neither said anything.

Finally, with a faint smile on his face, Daniel said, "Would you like to dine with me my darling?

She took him by the arm and they went inside.

🕷

Daniel didn't really know where to begin, so he decided to start at the beginning.

"Are you aware that your birth was the result of in vitro fertilization?" he asked her.

"Of course," she answered. "My parents had been trying for years to have a baby, but with no success. I always thought it was kind of special to have parents who wanted so much to have a child. Not every kid is so lucky."

"Did you also know that the embryo that was implanted in your mother came from a donor couple?"

"Yes. My mother explained that to me when I was quite young. I also thought that was extraordinary—that two people should do such a noble and generous thing. I have thought about them often throughout my life. My mother also told me I have siblings since the donor couple already had children, though there was an understanding right from the start that this whole matter was to remain completely confidential, and I have always respected that."

Daniel said, "Well you do have siblings but they are younger than you, but wait I am getting ahead of myself."

Olivia look at Daniel so puzzled but not concerned.

Daniel decided to recount the two conversations he'd had with her father, beginning with the one that took place at London Acute Care just after Olivia came out of her coma.

He told her of that day in December 1980, when a woman calling herself Mary Wagner had come into her father's office in Althorp with a man who was identified only as her driver Phillip. The woman explained that the purpose of the visit was because of her future parents-in-laws' insistence on knowing that she had no fertility issues before she and her fiancé could be married. There was also a stipulation that all embryos were to be destroyed.

"I'm shocked," said Olivia. "The story I grew up with was a lie?"

"It was the lie your father told your mother," he explained. "As far as we know, and I believe it, your mother never knew anything beyond what she told you."

"But, why?" Olivia came back. "Why would my father do that?"

Daniel went on to explain that, according to Arthur Franklin's story, Olivia's mother had grown so despondent that she'd attempted suicide, and on the day that Mary Wagner showed up, he made an impulsive, highly unethical and illegal decision to use one of Mary Wagner's fertilized eggs to impregnate her mother. "And on September 5, 1981, you were born," Daniel concluded.

"Oh my god! That's a lot to take in," Olivia exclaimed. "But what does any of that have to do with the attack on me?"

Daniel got up from his seat, as if to serve himself a piece of cheese, when in actuality he was trying to carefully choose his words for the next part of the story.

"So, the attack has something to do with the discovery by someone that I was the biological child of Mary Wagner and whoever it was that had donated the semen," Olivia deduced.

"That is our working assumption," Daniel answered.

"But, who? And again, why?"

"You might want to get a firm grip on your seat here, love."

Daniel then proceeded to tell her that a couple of months later, February 24th to be exact, her father saw the woman who had called herself Mary Wagner on BBC News, all smiling and beautiful for the announcement of her engagement to Prince Charles . . . Mary Wagner was Diana Spencer.

Olivia sat in her chair paralyzed for almost two minutes and then almost like in slow motion she headed for the Bombay. She didn't say a word as she poured herself straight gin in a tall glass. She appeared to Daniel to be processing this information with that brilliant mind of hers.

Returning to the table, she served them both some salad and sat quietly for a minute.

Finally, she spoke.

"So, let me get this straight," she began rather calmly. "It is your belief, based on a conversation with my father and whatever investigative work the police have done, that I am the biological child of the Prince and Princess of Wales, the older sister of Princes William and Harry?"

Daniel just nodded.

"Oh dear god!" shouted Olivia, before downing her entire glass of gin. "Daniel, if this is true, it is almost unfathomable," said Olivia. "How am I supposed to take this? What does this mean? This must be a lie. What else do you know?"

"Not much, I'm afraid," Daniel answered. "And way more than I think I can handle right now."

Daniel's expression was a mixture of fear and sadness, and Olivia got really scared.

"JESUS CHRIST!" she said in a moment of understanding. "You know who tried to kill me—someone who recently found out about my existence and wants me dead—someone who's trying to protect the Royal Family from a scandal that would rock the world and possibly jeopardize the monarchy itself—someone who needs every trace of this matter to go away. I must call my father. I need to hear what he has to say. I am sure this is a mistake and there is a reasonable explanation for this mess?"

Daniel sat almost frozen and silent.

Olivia analyzed the situation for another minute, and then it dawned on her.

"Oh, no," she finally said, tears streaming down her face. "Daniel, please, please! Tell me it isn't so. Not my parents!"

Daniel rose from his chair, and moved to Olivia, lifting her into his arms. All he could do was hold her.

"I'm so sorry, sweetheart," he said after a bit. "I know you loved them very much —as much as they loved you."

"Oh, god, Daniel. Oh, my god."

After what seemed like hours of consoling her—hugging and kissing and growing ever closer, Olivia pulled away to ask the obvious question.

"How did they die?"

"An explosion at their home last night. They died instantly, Olivia."

After pacing around the room for several minutes, Olivia's mood suddenly changed completely: from grief to anger.

"Who the hell did this, Daniel? And why now?"

Daniel recounted the second conversation that he and Chief Inspector Armstrong had had with Olivia's father just before he was killed.

" . . . And near the end of the reception, you were engaged in conversation with a man in uniform. Do you remember that?"

"I do," she answered quickly. "His name is Phillip Churchill—a member of the Queen's Royal Guard."

"Head of the Royal Guard," Daniel told her.

"Go on," said Olivia, sensing something was lurking just around the next corner.

"Near the end of your conversation, your parents came over and you introduced them to Churchill. Your father, according to what he told me on the very night he died, immediately recognized Churchill as the man who had been 'the driver' for Mary Wagner all those years ago. What's more, he was quite sure Churchill recognized him."

"So you think Churchill put two and two together and decided that we must all be eliminated?"

"That's our current thinking," Daniel answered.

"Oh Daniel, Lt. Churchill even commented to me that I reminded him of Princess Diana. It didn't surprise me since all my life I had been told that. He said that from the back I could have been her double, my height, etc. He also said that he knew the Princess very well and looking into my eyes was like looking into hers. I was flattered and just thanked him," Olivia whimpered.

"Do you think there may be anyone else involved?" Olivia whispered.

"Not to our knowledge," he said, "but we're a bit thin on information at this point."

"Well, why can't the police just pick up Churchill and see what they can get out of him?" asked Olivia.

"Because the police have nothing—no witnesses, no physical evidence, just the word of a dead man."

"So, where does that leave us?" Olivia asked him. "We can't just keep running because my life's in danger, and I'll be damned if I'm going to let my parents' murderer or murderers get away with this. Shit! I should be in London right now making funeral arrangements."

"Your Uncle Thomas is handling that," Daniel told her. "Armstrong spoke to him this morning, and you'll be able to speak with your aunt and uncle tomorrow after I hear from Armstrong, sometime before noon."

"So, there's nothing to do for the moment except to sit tight," she realized.

Daniel said nothing. He just watched her pace around the room, knowing full well that her cerebral computer was analyzing a ton of data.

After a few minutes, she turned to him with those familiar eyes that had long ago made her so positively captivating. Now, her eyes glistening with tears and had the look of defeat.

Chapter Nine

After Daniel's revelation neither Daniel nor Olivia could swallow another bite of food, including an amazing chocolate soufflé and a crème brulée that was simply magnificent, but now not even a thought. Daniel asked Olivia if she would be ok if he took a shower. She hardly heard him, and just gave him a faint smile.

While he did so, Olivia disposed of most of what was left of their dinner, using the plastic laundry bags in the closet to conceal an appropriate amount of uneaten food so Marcel would not be insulted.

Daniel stood in the shower for a very long time, just letting the soothing water wash the stress of the day from his entire being.

When he got out, Olivia was naked and waiting in bed. The gin had really relaxed her and also numbed her thoughts.

Daniel promptly joined her, propped himself up on his left elbow, and simply stared at her face.

"My god!" he finally said, "Do you have any idea how gorgeous you are?"

"You might want to get your eyes checked, Doc. I can recommend a good

ophthalmologist."

"No, I mean it. I don't think I've ever noticed how truly stunning you are."

"It's still an eye thing, Daniel. You are merely looking at me through the eyes of a man in love," she explained.

"Does that mean I've gotten more handsome?" he asked teasingly.

"Well, in your case, it's a little different," she answered.

"How do you mean?" he asked, propping himself up a bit more.

"Well, for me it's not a matter of handsome or more handsome, or suddenly looking like Adonis. For me, you are simply the most beautiful man I've ever met," she explained. "You are bright, sensitive, caring, noble, and if your vanity truly demands it, I don't mind telling you that you are unquestionably the best looking guy in all of Calais. Now kiss me, you fool."

The kiss was long and deep and slow—not like the fiery kisses they had shared earlier. It was clearly Daniel's intention to take Olivia to that place where tenderness, desire, and sexual fulfillment are suddenly one.

She was now lying in the crook of his left arm as the fingers of his right, along with a thousand soft kisses showered her lips, her cheeks, and entire face. Sometimes he would kiss her mouth more intensely, as his right hand moved ever so gently along her neck, shoulders, and chest. It was almost as though his hand was scouting her body in advance of his mouth. This was uncharted territory, and Daniel fully intended to examine every bit of it with his caresses and kisses. It was a slow journey over an exquisite landscape that he would explore in every detail.

He took his cues from her whispered sighs and moans as he moved across her body—the underside of her chin, her breasts and nipples, her hips and tummy, her thighs and calves, all ten of her toes, one by one. As he moved his hand ever so slowly over her left leg, behind her knee, and up her inner thigh moving ever so gradually. His hand guided with the skill of the greatest lover building Olivia's excitement with such intensity. Her sighs grew louder and more frequent with the pressure of his fingers.

Gently stroking, her wetness drove him nearly insane—softer, harder, massaging her. As she bit down on the corner of her pillow, Daniel replaced his fingers with his mouth working his tongue introducing her to excruciating ecstasy.

"Oh, god!" she said.

"Oh, Daniel."

"Oh, my god, Daniel!" she said even louder.

"My god!" she shouted.

"Oh, my god, Daniel, I love you so!" she screamed as her body suddenly arched and then relaxed.

"I love you, too," he whispered. "And I am yours completely, Olivia."

He held her for a long time, just stroking the wet locks of hair that clung to her forehead, kissing her over and over, and repeatedly whispering, "I am yours, love. I am yours completely."

After a time Olivia said, "Dr. Whittemore, you have amazing hands."

"Well, I am, after all, a specialist," he responded. "And I must tell you, my dear, you have yet to see all my 'tools', or my full range of techniques."

She giggled and turned toward him.

"And is there anything I can do for you, love?"

He hugged her ever so lovingly and said, "You already have, sweetheart. More than you could possibly know. You already have."

They drew each other close, all tangled up with one another in silence and darkness. Soon, they were both asleep.

At precisely 8:00 the following morning, Nigel Prescott arrived at Edward Armstrong's office at Scotland Yard.

"Coffee?" Armstrong offered.

"No thanks," Prescott answered. "I've already had a couple of liters this morning, and I'm not due for a fill-up for at least twenty minutes."

"So, Eddie-boy," Prescott continued, "What's this bloody farce all about?"

"I'm going to tell you Nigel, but you have to promise me that what is said in this room will stay in this room."

"No bloody chance," said Prescott. "All I can do is assure you I will play it by the book and make my own judgments," he explained.

"Well, I guess that will have to do," Armstrong replied. "But, will you please indicate your intentions after this meeting?"

"As sure as a dart in flight, Eddie," he came back.

"Fair enough," said Armstrong,

Chief Inspector Armstrong then proceeded to tell his friend everything he knew relating to Olivia, her parents, Whittemore, Churchill, the events of the previous days—the whole bloody mess—and Prescott proceeded to jump in now and again to ask a question.

"So, that bit with Gatwick and the Chunnel was all a ruse," he commented.

"That's correct," Armstrong answered.

"And the stuff about them using credit cards and buying tickets—the stuff Smitty gave us?"

"All of it true, and all of it planned to come off exactly as it did."

"And I suppose you are in communication with Whittemore and the girl?" Prescott asked him.

"That I am," said Armstrong.

Nigel sat back in his chair for a moment, just mulling it all over.

"I think I'll have that coffee now," he said casually.

"Down at the end of the hall," Armstrong told him. "If you don't mind . . ."

"Cream and sugar?" Prescott asked, rising from his chair.

"Black, please," Armstrong answered.

"So, you think this toss-pot Churchill is behind everything and using us to try and locate Olivia to have her done in?" Prescott speculated.

"And we've been using our resources to send the RMP off-course to keep Olivia and Daniel out of harm's way . . . at least until we can deal with Churchill," Armstrong answered.

Prescott mulled a bit more then speaks. "Tell you what I think, Eddie," he began. "First of all, I believe this whole sod story, just as you've told it; second, I think this was supposed to be a one-man job until Churchill botched the murder of the girl and had to bring in a few cronies to help him find her. They probably know nothing beyond that cock and bull story about the IRA; finally, I think Lt. Colonel Churchill is way out of his league and that sooner or later—probably sooner—he's going to screw up the whole affair. Problem is, right now we've got nothing on him."

"So, what would you suggest as a course of action?" Armstrong asked him.

"Well, first there are a few questions I'd like to put to him, namely why didn't he go outside the RMP when he first got this so-called terror alert. Next, I'd like to ask him where he was on December 24, 1980, just to see his reaction," Prescott said with a smile.

"I also think we need to keep up the good cop/bad cop thing," Armstrong suggested. "He seems to trust you and prefers to talk to you. Besides, I think there's a good chance he may have recognized me from the night he blew up the Franklin's house."

"By the way . . . have you seen this?" Armstrong asked as he slid that morning's edition of the *Times of London* across his desk.

Prescott scanned and then read aloud.

"The fire, which was originally thought to be the result of a faulty gas stove, is now being called a 'deliberate bombing' according to RMP Major Richard Ripley, who's been investigating the case. According to Ripley, 'The device that was used was a sophisticated bomb that has been associated with the IRA for a number of years. We believe this one was set by a splinter group called 'The Real Brotherhood.' Ripley explained."

"Blimey!" said Prescott, pounding his fist on the paper.

"It goes on to say that the likely target was Olivia Franklin, a suspected defector from the Real Brotherhood," Armstrong explained.

"Bastards," Prescott shouted. "What time are those wankers going to be here?"

"Another forty minutes," said Armstrong, looking at his watch. "That is, if they show at all."

"Well, here's what I'm thinking," said Prescott, looking pretty riled.

Chapter Ten

Churchill and his men arrived at Armstrong's office a little after 10:00 a.m.

"And how are we all this fine lovely morning?" he began.

Prescott and Armstrong just stared at each other.

"Hmm. Tough night, eh, mates?" he added before taking a seat.

Extra chairs had been brought in to accommodate Majors Ripley, Wright, and two other men who were quickly introduced as Majors Blackstone and Townsend.

"Let's cut the chitchat Lt. Colonel Churchill," said Armstrong with a glower on his face. "In the first place, you can drop the royal 'we,' and I am neither fine nor lovely this morning. Oh, and I believe I can speak for Inspector Prescott when I say that we are definitely not your mates."

"Ah, excuse me Eddie," said Prescott, jumping in. "Colonel, we just need to clear up a couple of things," he said, turning to Churchill. "Sir, what can you tell us about this IRA plot that seems to be at the root of this whole business?"

"The one you failed to mention when we bumped into you at London Acute Care on the morning of the 26th?" Armstrong added.

"I believe I said it was classified at the time," Churchill answered.

"And now?" asked Prescott.

"Well it's still quite sensitive," said Churchill.

"Sensitive," Armstrong repeated. "So sensitive that it's all over the morning papers?" he asked while tossing his copy of the Daily Mail to Ripley.

Churchill jumped from his chair and said quite indignantly, "Listen, Armstrong, I don't know what kind of nasty bug has flown up your arse this morning, but I will not stand for this kind of treatment."

"Good," said Armstrong, "then sit your arse back down in that chair and keep your trap buttoned until you are spoken to."

Anticipating the likely response from Churchill and his men, Armstrong pressed a button on his desk and his door swung open, revealing a small mob of elite detectives called "Scuffers" holding automatic weapons.

"Something we can do for you, Chief Inspector?" asked one of the policemen.

"Yes, Jimmy. Just see that no one leaves or enters this room until I give the say-so," instructed Armstrong.

Everyone stood in shock as the door closed.

"This is insane," said Ripley, trying the locked door.

"You have no right to do this," said Major Blackstone.

"This is outrageous," said Churchill. "Your superiors will hear of this, I assure you," he added, wagging a finger at Armstrong.

"Are you sure that's what you want, Lt. Colonel Churchill?" Prescott asked calmly.

Churchill paused a little too long and then sat back down in his chair and signaled his men to do the same.

"Okay, so is there a way we can do this calmly?" Churchill said diplomatically. "We are, after all, on the same team, you know." (Something he shouldn't have said, it only angered Armstrong.)

Armstrong looked at Prescott, who nodded.

"Gentleman," Armstrong said in an even-tempered voice. "I'm going to give it to you straight and true, and I really hope you listen closely because there will be no Q&A when we're through."

They all shifted uneasily in their seats, but no one spoke.

"First of all," Armstrong began, "I want you all to know that we have the greatest respect and admiration for your service to the crown. The security you provide to the homes and persons of the Royal Family is unequalled in this world."

Churchill rolled his eyes.

"I have a very special admiration for the way you are trained in matters of etiquette and protocol, and your exceptional commitment to isolating the Royals from gossip, impropriety, inappropriate behavior, scandal, and the like. The reputation and public persona of the House of Windsor must remain beyond reproach at all times. I can imagine that there are certain occasions when one must go to great lengths—extreme lengths, to maintain those standards."

"Is this leading up so something?" asked Churchill, quite aggravated by the current discourse.

"Yes it is, Sir," he answered, staring directly into Churchill's eyes. "Let me ask you then, when was the first time you met Olivia Franklin?"

"What? I've never met her in my life," Churchill answered.

"And her father, Arthur Franklin . . . have you ever met him?"

"What are you talking about, Armstrong?" Churchill shouted, his face as red as the Thames at sunset.

"Did you attend a charity function for the Childhood Cancer Research Group in February?" Prescott asked him.

"Do you know or have you ever known a woman named, Mary Wagner?" Armstrong asked him before he could answer Prescott's question.

Churchill rose to his feet.

"You better be careful, gents. You don't know what you're dealing with here."

"Oh, I think we know quite a bit more than you think," said Armstrong before pushing the button on his desk.

"We're done talking, Philly-boy. I already know what you've been up to."

The door swung open and the same bobby as before said, "Something we can do for you, Inspector?"

Armstrong simply stated, "Yes, Jimmy. Would you please escort Lt. Colonel Churchill from the building and have him delivered to the destination of his choice."

"Certainly, Sir," Jimmy replied, and in barely an instant, Churchill was whisked from the room, screaming obscenities as he went. His deputies, under threat of force, remained in place.

"So, what now?" said Ryan Wright, assuming the leadership role.

"First of all," Armstrong began. "I want you to know that I meant everything I said about protecting the Royal Family from scandal. That is, in fact, what this whole thing is about."

"I don't get it," said Ripley. "Can you explain?"

Armstrong looked at Prescott, who glanced at his notes and then said, "Mr. Ripley, who told you that the explosion at the Franklin's home was caused by a bomb that was suspected to have been planted by the IRA?"

"It was Lt. Colonel Churchill," Ripley answered.

"And did Lt. Colonel Churchill happen to tell you how he came by that information?" Prescott continued.

"He said he got it from the Knightsbridge bomb squad."

"And what if I was to tell you that there is no Knightsbridge bomb squad, and that no one in the whole of the London Fire Brigade knows anything about an IRA bomb—what would you say to that?"

Ripley said nothing.

"Tell me this then, when did you first hear about this IRA plot?"

"Last Sunday," Ripley answered. "The 6th, I believe."

"Within hours of the explosion at the Franklin's home," Armstrong pointed out.

"We didn't know about the explosion until the next day," Ripley answered.

"I would think not," said Armstrong.

"And do any of you know the name of the source in the IRA who gave Churchill this tip?" Prescott asked.

No one spoke.

"Mr. Townsend," Prescott continued. "What would you say if I told you that, despite what Lt. Colonel Churchill said earlier, he had met Arthur, Elizabeth and Olivia Franklin in February?"

"I believe I would ask you to provide evidence of such a meeting," Townsend replied.

"Would their signatures in a guest book at a charitable event be sufficient?"

"I think not," said Townsend.

"How about a number of credible witnesses who saw them together that evening?" Prescott continued.

Townsend said nothing.

"Mr. Blackstone," said Armstrong, "What do you think of all of this?"

"I'd say your implications are rather clear, but your case is less than thin," Blackstone answered.

"Would it help if I told you that I have video from a security camera at the hospital that shows Churchill and the Franklins conversing for several minutes at that charitable event on the 11th of February of this year?"

"What's going on here?" said Wright, rising from his chair.

Armstrong looked at Prescott who said, "Tell them."

Wright sat back down, hoping for a full briefing, which is pretty close to what he got.

"Let me begin by saying that there are only four people in the world who know about all of this—two are in this room, and the other two are in a place where they will never be found," Armstrong began. "Now, none of us have any desire to see this come out; to the contrary, we are all committed to ensuring that it never sees the light of day. Personally, I will be quite content if the attack on Olivia Franklin and the murder of her parents remain unsolved cases until the end of time. It is that important that this information never be made public."

"Excuse me, Inspector," said Wright. "This is all a little too cryptic for my tastes. I'm afraid you're going to have to give us a bit more."

"Nigel?" said Armstrong.

Inspector Prescott took a deep breath before saying what he was prepared to say.

"Several weeks ago, Lt. Colonel Churchill bumped into the Franklins at a charity event, and that set this all in motion. Without giving you details that I simply cannot divulge and still ensure that the matter remains known only to the four people who are in possession of the full story, I will tell you this. As a result of that chance encounter, Lt. Colonel Churchill became convinced that all three of the Franklins must be eliminated in order to guarantee that a most shocking and destructive threat to the monarchy be avoided."

"And I don't suppose you're going to tell us the nature of that threat?" said Wright.

"Obviously not," said Prescott. "But I can tell you that at this point, the only real threat here is Churchill and his bumbling actions, which have already drawn too much attention to this already."

"Just so we are clear here, you're telling us that Churchill attacked Olivia Franklin and then killed her parents?" asked Wright.

"That is precisely what we are saying," said Armstrong.

"So why did you let him go?" asked Ripley.

"Because, every moment we remain involved in this matter raises the likelihood that this will all come out," said Armstrong.

"So what are we supposed to do with all of this?" asked Wright. "Even if I did believe the tale, I'm not sure how I should proceed."

"Do whatever you have to do to bring this to an end," said Prescott. "But, know this:

If any harm should come to Olivia Franklin, Dr. Daniel Whittemore, Chief Inspector Armstrong, or myself, it will unleash a firestorm of controversy the likes of which England has not seen in a thousand years."

Armstrong pressed the button on his desk, and the door to his office swung open.

"Yes, Sir?" said the guard.

"These men are free to go," said Armstrong.

As the RMPs left the room, some of them scratching their heads, Armstrong and Prescott just stared at one another.

It was Prescott that spoke first.

"You think that will do it?" he asked.

"We shall see what we shall see," said Armstrong. "We'll know soon enough if they are with us or against us. In the meantime, I'm willing to bet they have more than a few questions for Lt. Colonel Churchill."

Chapter Eleven

Olivia and Daniel woke up to a glorious day. It was glorious before they got out of bed; glorious before they opened the curtains to see how really glorious it was outside; glorious in almost every respect. (Jeez! How glorious a day must be when it seems so glorious before you've even picked up a toothbrush?)

While Olivia was in the shower, she went over all of it in her head.

The first thing she thought about was her parents and how desperately they wanted to have and raise a child and what a wonderful job they had done. Olivia had a strong sense of self. She knew she was bright, empathetic, morally grounded, witty, clever, and a generally good person. She was not arrogant about any of that—her self-worth was rooted in gratitude, an appreciation of life and love and peace and happiness, and an awareness of pain and suffering in the world and her sense of responsibility, even obligation, to do whatever she could to lessen that pain and suffering that so many are afflicted with.

She attributed all of these qualities to her privileged upbringing by two loving and nurturing parents who raised her to be the person she is today. She missed them very much and was sure that would never change.

As she shampooed her hair, Olivia's thoughts shifted to Daniel.

It has been said that love born of an intense, shared experience is almost certain to fail. She wondered about that and the fact that, at the very moment such a huge void appeared in her life with the death of her parents, Daniel was there to fill so much of it with love and companionship. She believed that she and Daniel were truly perfect for one another, but her analytical brain was always looking for new data. Still, she had already decided to give herself to him completely, and she allowed herself to think it was the same for him.

And then there was the matter of Princess Olivia. She was still having a great deal of difficulty wrapping her brain around that one, but she was smart enough to know that sorting out that business must be a very high priority.

Chief Inspector Armstrong was still at his desk when his phone rang.

"Armstrong," he said, unceremoniously.

"Chief Inspector, this is Major Wright of the RMP," came the voice on the other end of the line.

"Yes, Major," said Armstrong. "What can I do for you?"

"I suspect you already know that Lt. Colonel Churchill has gone underground."

"What makes you say that?" asked Armstrong.

"Because he's not at the palace, not at his home, and he is not answering his cell," said Wright.

"So?" said Armstrong.

"So, I thought you would want to know that," said Wright.

"I certainly do," said Armstrong. "What I don't know is why you are calling to tell me that?"

"Chief Inspector, you may not believe this, but if what you said about Mr. Churchill is accurate, it is a matter of great concern to the RMP. Whatever his initial motivation was, his recent actions, if true, constitute a grave threat to the Crown."

"I can see that, Major Wright. What I don't see is how you plan to act on the information we have given you," said Armstrong.

"Well, therein lies the rub," said Wright. "We don't have the resources you have to follow up on this, whatever it maybe."

"So, are you proposing a partnership between Scotland Yard and the very people who have sworn their allegiance to Churchill? How's that going to work, Mr. Wright?"

"It begins with trust, Chief Inspector, and I am willing to do whatever is necessary to create a bond of trust between us."

"And how do you propose to do that, Major?"

"I have something that should be of great interest to you," said Wright. "And I'd like to swing by and share it with you."

"Come on over," said the Chief Inspector. "I'll leave my door unlocked."

Olivia and Daniel decided to have breakfast in the Meurice dining room. It was just a light breakfast of croissants, strawberry preserves, and café au lait. Neither of them, it turns out, were big breakfast eaters.

As if reading Olivia's mind, Daniel asked her about the subject that was foremost in her mind, her parents, but Olivia could not bring herself to talk about them.

"So, what do you think of this whole princess thing?" he asked instead.

"I've been trying to sort it out, without much success," she answered. "I need your help with this, Daniel."

"Anything I can do, of course. How can I be of assistance to you, love?" he asked.

"Just help me talk it through, Daniel. Sometimes that's the best way for me to get a handle on things."

"OK. First question: How does it feel to be the daughter of Prince Charles and Princess Diana?" Daniel asked.

"Conflicted," she answered. "On an intellectual level, it's fascinating—like something out of a fairytale. It's also somewhat titillating, enchanting, attractive, and bizarre. I mean, it was one thing to be told that I had biological parents and siblings who would remain forever unknown to me because of the circumstances of my birth. It is quite another thing, now that those 'facts' have changed. I am the biological daughter of a woman who I have always idolized but never met. I have a father and two brothers whose names I know; I know what they look like and some of the details of their lives—yet we've never met, and it seems unlikely that they even know I exist. What am I supposed to do with that?"

Daniel thought for a moment and then said, "Not to be glib, but what do you want to do with that?"

"To be frank," said Olivia, picking at her croissant, "I want to be acknowledged by my family, but I don't want to do it in any way that would ever be public."

"Why's that?" Daniel asked her.

"Well, for one thing, I don't want to live in a spotlight under a microscope. My father and brothers had no choice in that regard, but I have been given that choice. It's a lot to consider."

"So, answer me this," Daniel said to her. "What would constitute the ideal scenario for you?"

Olivia thought for a moment before answering. "I guess the ideal situation, which probably isn't possible, would be one in which I could have a relationship with my family without anyone else in the world ever knowing about it."

"That's a pretty tall order," said Daniel. "But sweetheart, listen to me." He locked eyes with her, getting her full attention. "Just because something is seemingly impossible, that does not mean one should fail to strive for it. What say, we try to develop a plan based on creating your ideal scenario, and see where it takes us?"

"I love you, Daniel. You're starting to feel like the rest of me. It's a feeling I can't get enough of."

"Let's go up and organize our day. I'm expecting an email anytime now from Eddie Armstrong."

Major Wright walked into Armstrong's office carrying a small attaché case.

"So, what is it that you want to share with me to begin building this bond of trust between us?" Armstrong began.

"Do you know where Mr. Churchill is right now?" Wright asked.

"Yes I do," Armstrong answered.

"Will you tell me?" Wright asked.

Armstrong thought for a moment before answering.

"He's at the Earl's Court Tavern," said Armstrong. "Been there since about 11:00 a.m." "And do you know if he is meeting with anyone there?" Wright pressed on.

"He's sitting in a booth with a man about 60 years of age, graying hair, looks pretty fit—they each have a pint of stout before them, which they have barely touched."

"And do you know who that man is, Chief Inspector?"

"No, I do not," said Armstrong. "Are you going to tell me?"

"His name is Hugh Dixon," the Major answered. "He's been Churchill's mentor throughout his career."

"And the significance of that is?" Armstrong asked with genuine interest.

"The significance of that is that they are deciding what Churchill should do. If he leaves that pub and goes back to the Palace or to his home, he will be assured by a member of the RMP that we and you, meaning Scotland Yard, are prepared to sweep this whole matter under the rug. And that will be the truth," Wright explained.

"And if he doesn't go home or to the Palace, or in some way indicates that this isn't over yet, then what?" Armstrong asked him.

"Then I am prepared to help you in any way I can to stop him," Wright answered.

"And just what kind of help would that be?"

Major Wright pulled a file from the attaché case he was carrying and placed it before Armstrong.

"This is Mr. Churchill's complete dossier," Wright began. "His whole life is in here. Addresses, telephone numbers, bank accounts, all family and known acquaintances since the day he was born."

"That would be quite useful, Mr. Wright. So now we just wait and see which way he turns?" Armstrong asked.

"That's about it," said Wright.

Armstrong extended his hand to Major Wright who immediately grasped it.

"Welcome to the team, Major," Armstrong said as they shook.

"For Queen and country," the Major answered.

When Daniel and Olivia returned to their room, there was an email from Armstrong that said the following:

Things are contained for the moment. Go enjoy a couple of days off. Have some fun. Make sure your cells are on at all times. Sherlock

Chapter Twelve

Armstrong was on the phone with Prescott, who had joined the surveillance teams in and outside of the Earl's Court Tavern.

"No, they haven't moved," said Prescott. "They've been sitting in that same booth for hours, just talking."

"Nothing else?" Armstrong asked.

"Churchill went to the loo one time, and Dixon has made and received several calls on his cell."

"Anyway to get ears on those calls?" Armstrong asked.

"I called the techies, and they're on their way," said Prescott.

"Alright. Keep me posted. But if either of those blokes leaves the pub, I want them followed, with frequent reports to me." Armstrong hung up the phone.

"What is going on?" said Armstrong to no one but himself.

At that same time, Olivia and Daniel were in the EuroStar station in Calais, awaiting their train to Paris. Aside from being one of Europe's most charming and romantic cities, Paris is a travel hub that is unequalled in the world. From Paris, they could travel by air, rail, auto, bus, boat, or bicycle to anywhere in Europe, and by ship and international flight to destinations all over the globe. They would arrive in the early evening, find a suitable hotel, and enjoy a few days enjoying each other.

Daniel was busy tapping away on his laptop, doing all kinds of research on hotels, travel options, museums, and the Royal Family. Olivia was making her first call on her new phone to her father's brother, Thomas.

"I'm okay, really," she told him. "Don't worry."

"Don't worry?" her uncle came back. "According to the phone call I got from that police inspector, Arthur and Elizabeth were murdered by someone who is also trying to kill you. How can we not worry under those circumstances?"

"Inspector Armstrong has assured me that things are under control," she told him. "He knows who's behind this and why, and he's building his case as we speak."

"If the situation is under control, as you say, then why can't you come to the funeral?" asked her uncle.

"It's complicated," Olivia answered. "Just know that I am safe and that I'll be home soon."

"Hold on. Your Aunt Helen wants to speak with you."

"Hello?" came the voice of Olivia's aunt.

"Hi, Aunt Helen. How are you holding up?"

"Not at all well, my dear. And I don't expect to be until I know what's going on. Where are you?"

"I can't tell you that, Aunt Helen. It's safer if no one knows my where-abouts," Olivia told her.

"Is that supposed to be reassuring, Liv? Because it's not."

"I'm sorry, Aunt Helen. Believe me; I am not thrilled about missing my own parents' funeral."

Olivia was suddenly overcome with grief and sadness and just wanted to curl up into a ball. She began to cry.

"Oh, Livy, I know how hard this must all be for you. It's hard on all of us. Just make me one promise, if you can."

"What's that?" asked Olivia.

"Just call in as often as you can to let us know you are okay. Can you do that?" Helen asked.

"I'll call you tomorrow," answered Olivia. "I have to go now, OK?" she said in a voice that was choked with emotion. "Tell Uncle Thomas goodbye."

Olivia laid her head on Daniel's shoulder and continued to cry as their train pulled into the station.

A few minutes later, Hugh Dixon's cell phone rang on vibrate on the table in the booth he was sharing with Churchill.

"Yes?" Dixon said into the phone.

"They're on their way to Paris—on the train by the look of it," said the man who had tapped Thomas Franklin's house phone and was now tracking the GPS on Olivia's cell.

"Good work," said Dixon. "I'll talk to you later."

"Paris," said Dixon, rising from his seat. A moment later, he and Churchill exited the pub.

"Armstrong," said the Chief Inspector, as he customarily did when answering his phone.

"They just left the tavern," said Prescott, "immediately following a call to Dixon's cell. I'm afraid the tech guys arrived just a little too late to listen in. What now?" he asked.

"Stay on both men for a while," instructed the Chief Inspector. "Until we know what's going on, we're like flypaper on their backs. Got it?"

"Yes, Sir," said Prescott.

Armstrong hung-up and immediately dialed another number.

"Wright. It's Armstrong. You wouldn't happen to have one of those comprehensive files on Hugh Dixon, would you?"

"Anticipating that request, I just had it couriered over to you. It should be there any moment."

"Good lad," said Armstrong, who promptly hung up the phone.

Upon leaving the tavern, Phillip Churchill shook hands with his friend and then hailed a cab. When the cab went north on Earl's Court Road and turned east on Cromwell, it appeared that he was headed home to his flat in South Kensington.

Dixon walked a few meters to the Earl's Court tube station and caught a northbound train.

Teams of detectives were following both men, the group tailing Dixon having the more difficult task. Prescott was on the team with Churchill, which did, in fact, follow him to his flat.

"He's inside his flat," said Prescott, reporting to Armstrong. "What do you want to do now?"

"Just sit tight for a while, and we'll see what happens. Be sure to assign someone to the rear exit and to the roof."

"Will do," said Prescott, before ending the conversation.

Hugh Dixon was a tall man, nearly 6'5". He was wearing a tan mac over gray trousers and a bright red hat that would make him easy to follow. The only problem is that, in surreptitious surveillance by foot, the person being stalked has the clear advantage. If aware that he is being followed, he can almost always elude his followers.

After switching trains several times, Dixon knew for sure that he was being followed. He looked at his watch, which read 6:05 p.m.

"Right on schedule," he said to himself.

A few minutes later, Prescott recognized Major Ryan Wright approaching Churchill's door. He watched him knock and, after a moment, enter the flat.

This he reported immediately to Armstrong.

"I don't know what to say, Ryan," Churchill said to his number two.

They were facing each other from plush chairs in Churchill's sitting room.

"I think we should talk about this," said Wright.

At 6:25 p.m., Dixon and his pursuers arrived at palatial Victoria Station.

It was the height of rush hour, and in just a few minutes, Dixon would make his move based on information he had received during one of the afternoon's phone calls. The call had come from his granddaughter, Cat, a beautiful 19-year-old who was studying to be a dental technician.

After a few minutes of conversation with Wright, Churchill rose from his chair and said, "I don't know about you, Ryan, but I could use a stiff drink. Care for something?"

As Ryan begged off, Churchill moved to the liquor cart that stood against the wall behind Ryan's chair.

"Are you sure?" he asked, as he produced a silenced forty-five and fired two shots into the back of the Major's head.

A moment later, Churchill was on the phone with the London Fire Brigade to report a fire at his address.

Then, amid the chaos and din of the arriving fire trucks, their lights flashing, and sirens screaming, he opened his back door and fired three shots into the chest of a momentarily distracted bobby. Churchill then casually walked down the alley and around a corner.

At precisely 6:30 p.m., a portable sound system brought to Victoria Station by some college kids began to blare the song *Dancing Queen* by ABBA, and four thousand students participating in a pre-arranged flash mob broke into song and dance.

In less than two seconds, Hugh Dixon moved behind one of the giant steel pillars that support the station's glass roof, shed his coat and cap, and danced his way into the crowd.

Chapter Thirteen

Any good travel guide for Europe will tell you all you need to know about cell phone dead zones and Wi-Fi hotspots, unless you're trying to access that information while riding on a high-speed train.

This was a source of great frustration and concern to Chief Inspector Edward Armstrong, who'd been trying to contact Daniel and Olivia since the disappearance of Churchill and Dixon. It was also a problem for Daniel and Olivia, who had hoped to get a lot of research done on the train ride from Calais to Paris.

"Are you able to connect to the Internet?" Daniel asked Olivia.

"No. There's no connection." Olivia then reached for her cell phone and called Daniel, who was sitting in a seat that was facing her. The phone rang once, then nothing. "No phone, either," she said.

"Isn't it amazing how dependent we've become on these devices?" he commented.

"Not just us," Olivia answered. "Most of the world."

"I guess we'll just have to communicate face to face," Daniel said with a smile.

There was no one else sitting near them on the half empty train—a good thing, since their conversation quickly turned to Olivia's *Ideal Scenario.*

"I don't see any way to do this without contacting a member of the Royal Family in a credible way," Olivia said.

"A letter?" Daniel suggested.

"To whom? Saying what?" Olivia responded. "A letter to any one of the Royals going to be read first by a secretary, which immediately widens the circle of the number of people who know anything about this. Besides, what would it say?

Dear Prince William, It is very important that I meet with you at an isolated and completely secure location, with no one else present, so I can tell you about something very important that I can't discuss in a letter.

Respectfully, Anonymous

How far do you think that would get us, Daniel?"

"I see your point," Daniel responded. "There really is no way to do this by letter, no matter how cleverly worded."

They sat for a few moments in complete silence.

"I really don't see any viable options here," Daniel finally said. "You can't write them, call them, email them, approach them in public . . . what does that leave?"

"It would have to be through an intermediary," Olivia suggested.

"Who? Do you know someone you can trust with your life that has that kind of one-on-one access to any of the Royals?" asked Daniel.

"I was sort of hoping you did," she answered.

Daniel thought for moment before speaking.

"Listen," he began, leaning forward and taking Olivia's hands in his. "Just because we can't think of an intermediary doesn't mean we can't create one."

"How do you mean?" Olivia asked.

"We put our heads together and come up with a name—someone we don't yet know of—someone we can identify and attempt to contact confidentially with a likelihood of being successful—someone who can then access one of the Royals one-on-one."

"I'm not sure I follow," said Olivia looking puzzled.

"Well, even the Royals have friends—people they trust, people who can get together with them from time to time. A lifelong friend and confidant."

"I get it," said Olivia. "Like someone William or Harry grew up with, or maybe a friend of Kate Middleton's. But, wait. How do we do that?"

"Google," said Daniel. "You can find anything on Google."

They both leaned forward and kissed.

Chief Inspector Armstrong was cloistered in his office with Inspector Prescott and Majors Ripley, Blackstone and Townsend. Sitting before him on his desk was the dossier on Hugh Dixon that Major Wright had couriered over.

"Gentlemen," Armstrong began, "Let me first thank you for meeting with me after such a long and hectic day." Everyone just nodded. "Second, and more importantly," addressing the three RMP majors, "I want to express my sincere condolences for your loss. I didn't know Major Wright for very long, but I knew him to be a fierce patriot and a fine man."

"None better," said Ripley. The others wholeheartedly agreed.

"Chief Inspector, if I may," said Townsend. "We are all experiencing multiple levels of grief, confusion, dismay, and utter bewilderment. Our friend, Ryan, whom we all knew well, was murdered today, apparently by a man we have all worked with and respected for many years. This man who appears to be engaged in an incomprehensible plot with a distinguished, retired RMP who is something of a legend in the service, as well as being a man we all know and admire. I just don't know what to make of that, Sir."

"Neither do I, Mr. Townsend," said the Chief Inspector. "Even with all that I know about Mr. Churchill's apparent motivations—information, as I've said, that I simply can't share the whole of with you; I am stunned, confounded, and at something of a loss."

"None of it makes sense," said Major Blackstone. "What situation, potential scandal, whatever, could possibly cause Lt. Colonel Churchill to attempt to murder a private citizen of high standing, and then actually murder two other citizens, and then a member of his very own RMP and an MPS constable? It's unthinkable! What's more, it stretches the imagination beyond my limits to think that Churchill could then enlist the aid of the most honorable Lt. Colonel Hugh Dixon, one of the most loyal and esteemed members of the Queen's Guard in our entire history? What are we missing, inspectors?"

Prescott leaned forward in his chair and said, "I, for one, don't know the answers to any of those questions, but I am sure of one thing, Mr. Blackstone: we are missing something, and until we identify that something, none of this will make any sense."

There was a knock at the door, and Inspector Michael (Smitty) Smith entered and was quickly introduced to the RMP Majors.

"Inspector Smith runs our electronic surveillance and data analysis division—phones, computers, security cameras, all things tech," said Prescott.

"What have you got for us, Smitty?" Armstrong asked.

"Not much, I'm afraid," said Smitty. "Churchill has not used his cell since he left this office. He made one call from his home phone to the London Fire Brigade, and nothing since. We weren't quick enough to get ears on Dixon's phone calls from the Earl's Court Tavern, but we have since called the cell phone number listed for Dixon in his dossier, and though it hasn't been answered, we are fairly certain that it will see no further use."

"What brings you to that conclusion?" Armstrong asked Smith.

"Because the GPS on that phone shows that it's still in the tavern," he answered.

"So, let's review the last eight hours," said Armstrong.

"At approximately 10:20 in the morning, Churchill leaves this office and goes to the Earl's Court Tavern where he meets with Dixon."

"How'd he arrange that?" Prescott asked.

"He didn't have to," explained Major Blackstone. "He knew Dixon would be there."

Armstrong flipped through Dixon's dossier, and there it was.

"He owns the place," he said. "Okay, so Churchill goes to see his old friend, Dixon, and then what?" asks Armstrong.

"They sit in a booth all day, talking about who knows what, and Dixon makes and receives several phone calls, none of which we captured," Prescott said while glancing at Smitty.

"We didn't know who he was meeting at first, and by the time we got there, it was all over."

"Unfortunate, but understandable," said Armstrong. "So what can we surmise?" he continued.

"Churchill went to confer with an old and trusted friend about a very dicey situation," said Blackstone. "Whether it was to get advice, ask for help, or chew the fat, we have no way of knowing," he added.

"Well, let's assume for the moment that it was to enlist him in a conspiracy. Does that tell us anything about the phone calls?" asked Armstrong.

Prescott spoke first. "The phone calls he made—my notes say there were three—could have been to make arrangements, talk to someone who could aid them in their plans, try to get information on the whereabouts of Whittemore and Franklin—"

"Or, to talk to someone higher up," said Ripley, interrupting Prescott.

They all looked at Ripley with dismay.

"That would go a long way toward explaining how any of this is conceivable in the first place," offered Major Townsend.

"But, who would have that kind of influence over the top echelon of the Royal Guard?" asked Chief Inspector Armstrong.

The RMP Majors all looked at each other with dire expressions.

On a private yacht chartered out of the Brighton Marina, Hugh Dixon, a former Royal Marine and longtime recreational sailor, set course for La Havre. The charter had been arranged earlier in the day by a third party, who was unknown to him. On Churchill's instructions, the GPS autopilot was locked on to the Port de Plaisance Marina, which was some hours away. There had been no customs to clear when he and Churchill had set out from Brighton, nor would there be any when they landed in France.

From the information they'd gotten from Rousseau's man in London, they knew that the targets were headed to Paris by train; while Daniel and Olivia would certainly get there well before Churchill and Dixon, the GPS in Olivia Franklin's phone was all their man in the Sûreté would need to keep track of their whereabouts.

"Your story is quite remarkable," said Dixon to Churchill as they sat in the galley drinking tea.

"I can hardly believe it myself," said Churchill. "It was bizarre from the start, in my view, but a member of the Queen's Guard, as you well know, is not at liberty to question orders from the Royals."

"I understand that, of course, but how could you let this escalate to the point where people are being murdered?" asked Dixon.

"I know, I know," said Churchill looking quite forlorn. "But when I saw the girl, and then her father, all I could think of was how badly I had mishandled the original mission by not insisting to be present for the destruction of embryos, thereby allowing the surrogate birth of Charles and Diana's daughter. What can I say? When I saw Olivia and thought about what a nightmare this could create were she to ever learn of her royal lineage, I panicked. Then everything spun out of control."

"I understand that," said Dixon, "but how is it possible that you still feel compelled to pursue this?"

"Orders," said Churchill.

Just at the moment, the ship to shore radiotelephone rang.

"I'm pretty sure that's for you," said Churchill.

Dixon was completely mystified as he moved to the phone.

"Yes . . . yes it is . . . I understand . . . yes, of course . . . absolutely, Sir . . . yes, you can rely on me . . . certainly, Sir . . . goodnight, Your Royal Highness."

Just as the train from Calais was pulling into Gare du Nord, one of Daniel's pre-paid international cell phones rang.

"Yes," he said.

"It's me," said Armstrong, who was still in his office with the other investigator and the RMP Majors.

"Good to hear your voice," said Daniel. "How are we doing?"

"There have been some setbacks," Armstrong answered. "Churchill has disappeared; he may have one or more accomplices, and it's possible that they have knowledge of your whereabouts."

"How can that be?" said Daniel.

"Have either you or Olivia used your phones?" Armstrong asked.

"Let me think," said Daniel. "My phone, no, well, actually kind of. Olivia tried calling me when we were on the train but she didn't get through. No signal."

"Has she used her phone on other occasions?" Armstrong asked.

"Well, yes," said Daniel. "She used it to call her aunt and uncle—the ones who are making the funeral arrangements."

"That's it," said Armstrong. "Hold on a minute."

Armstrong explained to the others about the call to Thomas and Helen Franklin, and suggested that they put a guard on the Franklin's home just to be sure they were safe.

"Smitty, you go too, and see if you can discover anything." Then, returning to his phone call, "Daniel, we have to assume that those phones have been compromised. My phones are all secure and constantly debugged. We should use the phone you are on now only for communication between the two of us. So far as the other phones, this is what I want you to do."

"Okay, I've got it," Daniel said to Armstrong before ending the call.

"What's going on?" asked Olivia, sounding rather alarmed.

"No time to explain just now," Daniel answered. "Here's what I want you to do. Go into that gift shop over there, buy several things and pay for them with your Barclaycard. Then I want you to use your phone to call me on my phone and ask me where I am. Then, just follow my lead."

"Got it," said Olivia, turning towards the gift shop. "I guess," she muttered to herself.

Daniel moved to a position where he could see the monitors that listed arrival and departure times for all trains. He glanced at his watch. It was almost 9:30 p.m. After a couple of minutes, he saw what he was looking for. Shortly after that, his phone rang.

"Where are you . . . I step into the loo for one minute and you disappear."

"I popped into the gift shop to pick up a few things," said Olivia. "Where are you?

"I'm buying the tickets," Daniel told her. "Just stay at the entrance to the gift shop. I shouldn't be more than a couple of minutes," he said.

"I'll be here," she answered, and ended the call.

A few minutes later, after buying two tickets to Barcelona, Daniel grabbed Olivia by the arm and said, "We must hurry. We don't have much time."

"Don't have much time for what?" she asked.

"Could you please walk a little faster?" he responded, almost dragging her through the station.

A few minutes later, after boarding the train, Daniel said, "Give me your phone."

Without questioning him, she handed over the phone she'd been using and watched with interest as he checked to make sure it was on—then did the same thing to his own phone. He then dug them both in between the seat cushions and seat backs where they would not be seen.

"Come on," he said, "The train is almost ready to leave."

As they exited the Pullman car, a porter gave them a curious look.

"Forgot something," Daniel explained. "Just be a minute," he said before the two of them disappeared into the crowd.

Chapter Fourteen

After a good night's sleep and some good morning lovemaking, Daniel and Olivia were ready to hit the streets of Paris.

It was unusually warm and sunny for the second week of March, so they walked the thirty paces from the Hôtel du Rond-Point to the Champs-Elysees to get some breakfast and plan their day.

Check-in had been very easy at the modest hotel. They paid for a room for three nights using traveler's checks and informed the clerk that all other incidentals would be paid for in cash.

As they walked down the grand concourse, which many have called the most beautiful avenue in the world, they were feeling pretty good about how things were going. With a little luck, Churchill was on his way to Spain, and Daniel and Olivia just might get to enjoy a few peaceful days in one of the most romantic cities in the world.

"I love this place," said Olivia. "It just seems so . . . special."

"It is, indeed," said Daniel. "To think that seventy years ago this street was filled with German Panzer divisions and battalions of infantry."

"And look at it now," said Olivia. "Hitler never could have imagined that," she said, pointing to the denim-clad mannequins in the windows of the Gap.

They strolled the impressive promenade that stretches from the Place de la Concorde to the Place Charles de Gaulle, the site of the Arc de Triomphe. At its western end where they were, cinemas, theaters, cafés and luxury shops bordered the Champs-Elysées. Near the Place de la Concorde, the street was bordered by the Jardins des Champs-Elysées, beautifully arranged gardens with fountains and some regal buildings, including the Grand and Petit Palais at the southern side and the Elysée at its northern side. The latter has been the residence of the French Presidents since 1873.

"How about this place?" asked Olivia, pointing to a charming sidewalk café where they could get coffee and something to eat.

"Looks good to me," said Daniel.

Olivia was hungrier than usual and ordered a petit quiche and café au lait. Daniel also had the delicious French coffee, along with a brioche. The late morning sun felt good on their faces.

"So, what would you like to do today, love?" Daniel asked Olivia.

"Well, after breakfast, I'd like to do a little shopping," she answered. "It looks as if we may be on the road for a while, and I didn't bring enough clothes. I need some better walking shoes, some trousers, a couple of sweaters, and some thongs." She laughed as she continued. " I can probably get everything I need between here and the hotel."

"What do you need with thongs?" Daniel asked with a teasing smile on his face.

"Daniel, have you no shame?" she answered.

"Not when I'm with you, love," he answered. "And after the shopping? What then?"

"What I'd really like to do is go back to the room and get to work on that little project of ours," she answered.

"Project Google Princess," he said jokingly.

"That would be the one," she answered. "Only . . ."

"Only what?" Daniel asked.

"Only, we're going to have to give it a better name."

A little before dawn on that same morning, Dixon and Churchill tied up their chartered yacht at the Port de Plaisance Marina and went ashore. It had been a long day and night, with little sleep, and they still had much to do.

The first thing they did was call Rousseau in Paris.

"What do you have for us?" asked Dixon.

Rousseau related the information about the phone calls and the credit card usage at Gare du Nord, and the GPS signals they were tracking on a train destined for Barcelona.

"Barcelona?" Dixon said with surprise. "They're on a train to Barcelona?"

Churchill grabbed the phone from Dixon.

"This is Churchill," he began. "What makes you think they're headed for Barcelona?"

There was a long pause while Rousseau explained to Churchill about the GPS signals that they were picking up intermittently from the train.

"Have either of them made any calls since the train left Paris?" Churchill asked him.

"No, but there is little reception on the train," Rousseau explained.

"What about when the train makes stops? There should be good coverage at all the stations," Churchill said.

"No calls from either phone," answered Rousseau.

"Thank you. We'll get back to you in a few hours."

"What do you think?" said Dixon.

"I'm not buying this kettle of fish," Churchill responded.

"Why not?"

"These two are very savvy," Churchill said, pondering the situation. "You should have seen the wild chase they led us on to get out of England. They ran us every which way with false trails and misdirection. Plus they've got Scotland Yard assisting them every step of the way."

"But how can we know for sure?" asked Dixon. "They could be headed south or still in Paris, or gone off to who knows where."

"That is most certainly true," said Churchill, considering a range of possibilities.

"So, what do you want to do?" asked Dixon.

Churchill thought for a moment then said, "I'll explain it in the car."

Back in London, Armstrong and Prescott were pouring over the files they had on Phillip Churchill and Hugh Dixon.

"They have to be getting help from someone," said Armstrong.

"You mean someone higher up, like Ripley suggested?" said Prescott.

"That, too," said Armstrong.

"I'm not sure I'm following you, Eddie," said Prescott.

Prescott swiveled in his chair and looked directly at the Inspector.

"Ripley's theory makes sense," he began. "There probably is someone higher up who is issuing orders."

"You know what that means, don't you? The only higher ups in the case are the Royals," said Prescott.

"I know that," said Armstrong. "But it had to have been one of the Royals that had those fertility tests done in the first place. *Who*, is a matter of speculation."

"What I'm talking about," said Armstrong, returning to the files, "is someone else. Someone who is guiding Churchill and Dixon in their pursuit of Olivia."

"How do we even know they're pursuing Olivia? Could be they're just trying to disappear," said Prescott.

"That would be true if it was just Churchill, who was on the run because he knows that sooner or later, we'll have enough to get him for this. But I don't believe that's the case. The fact that both Churchill and Dixon took off immediately after that last phone call tells me there's someone else—someone with resources like we have to track Daniel and Olivia. No, Churchill didn't kill Wright and Constable Jackson just to get away. He did so because he was under orders from a Royal and because he's getting help from someone else."

"It makes sense," said Prescott. "I can't imagine any other circumstances than an order from above that would cause a man like Churchill to kill an RMP; why would he do so unless he had reason to believe he could be successful in his mission? That would require something like Scotland Yard, or Interpol, or some other sophisticated police organization."

"I believe that's the case," said Armstrong. "And I believe the answer to that question is somewhere in these files."

"Let's concentrate on Dixon," Prescott suggested. "It stands to reason that whomever this mystery person or agency or whatever it is, it was Dixon who somehow got them on board. After all, the 'go' signal went to him in that last phone call. How 'bout I make a copy of Dixon's file and we go through it line by line together?"

"Sounds like a plan," said Armstrong. "You make the copies, and I'll put on a fresh pot of coffee."

Daniel and Olivia were back at their hotel, each seated at their laptop. Like most hotels nowadays, the Hôtel du Rond-Point had free Wi-Fi in all rooms; and Google in France was the same as Google anywhere—except, maybe China.

"So, tell me again what we are looking for?" said Daniel.

"We are looking for someone we can easily approach, someone who has a close personal relationship with Charles, William, or Harry," Olivia explained.

"And does that beautiful mind of yours have a scheme for how we should go about this research?"

"As a matter of fact, it does," said Olivia with a proud smile. "I suggest we both work on the same Royal at the same time and compare notes. It's the most thorough way to go about it."

"So, who should we start with? Dad?"

A chill ran up Olivia's spine. "For some reason, that makes me uncomfortable," she said. "Let's start with the soon-to-be-wed young Prince—my brother, William."

"You got it," said Daniel. "Where shall we begin?"

"Let's start with pre-school and work our way forward."

⋔

Churchill and Dixon were driving in a Europcar rental from Le Havre to Paris. Dixon was behind the wheel of the gray Citroen, constantly reminding himself to stay on the right side of the road.

"If they are indeed on their way to Barcelona, your friend Rousseau should have confirmation for us soon," said Churchill. "Should that prove to be the case, we can fly from Paris to Barcelona and quite possibly get there in time to meet the train."

"And if they're not on the train," Dixon said, "we'll be at their last known location. Makes sense to me."

"How reliable is this Rousseau chap?" asked Churchill.

"He's as good a policeman as there is. I've known the man for over forty years. He operates a large, private investigative firm now but still has a lot of contacts within the Sûreté. He's told them that he's been hired by a wealthy English family to locate their daughter, who has run away with her lover, whom they do not approve of. His contacts are anticipating a considerable payoff when they are successful."

"Well, let's hope they are all amply rewarded for a job well-done," said Churchill.

⋔

His Royal Highness was pacing his quarters, looking much like a character out of a Shakespearean tragedy. His mood was dark and brooding, consumed with ominous thoughts.

It was he who had requested the fertility tests that started this royal mess, and he who would be at the center of the controversy should the facts ever become known. Yes, the knowledge of Olivia's existence had been the original motivation for Churchill's attack at the hospital. His

98

Highness understood that his loyal servant was only trying to protect the crown from what would certainly be a scandal of monumental proportion, were the people to find out that Diana had a daughter who preceded her sons. There would be arguments about succession; the debate over Diana's death would be rekindled; everyone from the Queen on down would be drawn into it.

But all of that had certainly been eclipsed by recent events. If it came out now that a member of the RMP had tried to kill Diana's daughter, it would rock the monarchy to an extent that he did not care to imagine.

His only hope was that the good doctor didn't know the whole story, and that if she did, she wouldn't go public. God forbid, if something like that were to happen.

Chapter Fifteen

Armstrong and Prescott, each with a pint of stout before them, sat in a corner of the Old Star Pub on Broadway, just a block from Scotland Yard. Spread out on the table was Dixon's dossier, thick and yellowed with age—a document that contained the whole of Lt. Colonel Dixon's career.

"I don't think we're making very much progress finding Dixon's man on the ground," said Prescott.

"It's here," said Armstrong. "I'm sure of it. His whole career is here. It has to be someone he's known for a long time, a trusted friend, someone who's plugged in."

"Plugged in to what—Scotland Yard, MI6, CIA, Interpol? I'm not seeing anything like that here," said Prescott. "Most of this is detail assignment. Guard this palace, provide security for the Duke and Duchess of So and So, travel arrangements, security abroad . . ."

"Excellent," said Armstrong. "Let's focus on trips abroad and someone he may have worked with in another police or intelligence service."

Armstrong took a swallow of his stout while rifling through pages of anything having to do with foreign travel or joint task forces.

"What do you think this is?" Prescott asked. He held a page up for Armstrong to see. "July 1967, Rousseau, Montreal," he read.

"I don't know," said Armstrong. "Is that all it says?"

"That's it . . . except for this handwritten notation—*Confidential Report delivered to HM, 29, July.*"

Armstrong sat back in his seat and scratched his head. Then he pulled out his secure cell and punched in a number.

"Smitty, I need you to do a comprehensive computer search using the following parameters . . . ready? Hugh Dixon, Montreal, July 1967, Rousseau. Yes, that's it . . . great, I'll see you then."

"We'll have it in the morning," Armstrong told Prescott. "If anyone can make sense of this, Smitty can."

Armstrong started to put away his cell but then remembered something.

"Blimey. I almost forgot. I have to send a text."

He tapped in the text message very carefully:

PHONES MAY HAVE BEEN COMPROMISED—MAKE NO FUR-THER CALLS—LEAVE PHONES ON TRAIN—FURTHER INSTRUC-TIONS TO FOLLOW VIA OTHER MEANS.

"Hey Eddie," Prescott said after his partner was done texting. "Does that HM bother you as much as it does me?"

"Are you finding this as frustrating as I am?" Olivia asked Daniel.

"I'm more surprised than frustrated," said Daniel. "You'd think with all the scrutiny the Royals get, it would be easier than this to find what we're looking for."

"It's like they have a pact with the press. Write what you will about us, but leave our friends out of it," Olivia commented. "I've just been through his entire experience at Eton, and I don't have even one possible yet."

"The problem is that everyone I'm finding would either be impossible to get to, or it's someone who is unlikely to have the prince's ear. I'm starting to wonder about this, sweetheart."

"No. It's here," said Olivia. "We just have to keep pressing."

Olivia kept tapping on her keyboard while Daniel just stared at her. 'How beautiful,' he thought. Not just her smile, those eyes, her hair, her amazing breasts, her shapely legs —Olivia was beautiful in ways that were so much harder to explain. Any man can make another man understand what he means by calling a woman a 'hot babe,' but how to explain a mind and a soul like Olivia's?

The woman was brilliant, and her brain worked like a computer, but her eyes, open or not, seemed to see things that most people never noticed or even care about.

Daniel had seen her on the ward, working with young cancer patients—little boys and girls, cruelly selected by fate or destiny or the roll of the dice to live in a world apart from the rest of us, a world of pain and uncertainty and fear. And then, Olivia walks into their topsy-turvy universe and they smile while they're crying, and they lock eyes with this gentile angel who knows, just knows, what is happening to them and that it's alright.

He'd seen it happen a dozen times. Olivia moves to the bed of a child only nine or ten, has awareness of their condition and what it's doing to their family and friends, what it means in the context of a rich, full life . . . and they look at Olivia and say, "How are you today, Miss?" My goodness!

"Sweetheart, you want to take a break, maybe go for a walk," he said to her.

"In a little while," she answered, without looking up from the screen of her laptop.

Churchill and Dixon were barely in Paris when they got the call from Rousseau about the text message. Without a lot of discussion, they made the decision to head to Charles De Gaulle Airport.

"I'm pretty certain that we can find a flight that will get to Barcelona before their train arrives," said Dixon. "If we can pick them up at the train station, our options will expand exponentially."

"I agree," said Churchill. "The best case scenario would be to spot them, tail them, and then make our plans to initiate the most efficient end to this."

"I think we can do that," said Dixon. "Once we have them on a short leash, we can create the optimal situation to deal with this."

"Do you have ideas in that regard?" asked Churchill.

"Just one," said Dixon. "We make them disappear without a trace. Dropped off the face of the earth, so to speak. No bodies to be found, no trail to follow, and you and me a thousand miles away."

"Perfect," said Churchill.

"Hugh," said Churchill. "You know I never would have drawn you into this, was it not for . . ."

"I understand, Phillip," said Dixon, cutting him off. "We chose an odd course for ourselves, and though it was a great honor and a grand life of privilege to live at the very center of the British universe, at the end of the day, our very complicated mission wasn't complicated at all. We swore our solemn allegiance to a singular idea —to serve the crown. That's all we have ever done with our lives, and that is what we are doing now. Nothing else matters."

"Thanks for that, Hugh. I've done some dreadful things that I can barely fathom; yet you just explained it as simply and eloquently as such a thing can be described. I truly appreciate that, my friend."

As they pulled up to the Iberia Airlines departure terminal, Churchill was almost numb in mind, body, and spirit. But the course was clear.

"Here, let me help you with that," Churchill said to Dixon, pulling the bags out of the boot of the car. He carried them to the curb and set them down.

Nothing was said as they hugged one another. Then Churchill walked to the car, got in, and drove away.

While most of London slept, Michael (Smitty) Smith was analyzing the data from his search.

"Cool!" he said to himself. "Armstrong's going to love this."

Chapter Sixteen

Daniel and Olivia were sitting on the love seat in their hotel room, all curled up in a tangle of arms and legs. It was past midnight, but neither of them wanted the day to end.

"So, Dr. Whittemore," Olivia began, "when did you first realize you were attracted to me?"

"That would be about four years ago, on the first day you walked into my classroom," he answered. "I took one look at you then suddenly realized I had stopped breathing."

"Are you saying I took your breath away?" Olivia quipped.

"That would be something of an understatement," Daniel answered. "It was as though the light in your eyes illuminated the whole operating theater. It was so bright, I could see nothing else. Just you."

"And when did you notice you were falling in love with me?" she asked him.

"That's a bit more tricky," he said, shifting his position a bit to better look into her eyes. "Attraction can happen in a millisecond. Call it pheromones or something else, there is an immediate physiological response that alters our whole biochemistry—our heart rate, hormone production—all sorts of things. Love, however, is a bit more nebulous, as authors and songwriters have pointed out for centuries. When was the moment I knew I was falling in love with you? Probably sometime after I had begun to do so. I just didn't admit it to myself until March 5th. And what about you, Dr. Franklin?" Daniel asked.

"Well, let's see," she began. "I would say it probably happened about 20 years ago."

"Come again?" said Daniel, a tad confused.

"I must have been about eight or nine. One day I just sort of realized that I was hopelessly and eternally in love with a man who was amazing in every way—his looks, his voice, his intellect, beliefs, moral anchors, the sound of his laughter, the sparkle in his eyes, the softness of his hands—I had a pretty clear picture of who this guy was; I just had to wait around until I met him."

"So, for you, too, it was your first day?" Daniel asked.

"No," Olivia responded. "Actually, it was about six months earlier. I attended a lecture you gave on pediatric trauma, specifically, rapid blood loss, internal and external, resulting from an acute insult to some part of the body."

"That's when you noticed you were falling in love with me?" said Daniel.

"No," Olivia explained. "That's when I noticed I was in a room with the man I'd been in love with since I was nine."

The statement was followed by a deep passionate kiss—the kind of kiss that people wait for all their lives.

Hugh Dixon and half a dozen of Rousseau's operatives were at Estacio de Franca in Barcelona. In a matter of minutes the train from Paris would be arriving, and each of the men spread out across the platform had pictures of Daniel and Olivia. They'd been warned to look for disguises, to expect that they might debark separately, and to be on alert for anyone even vaguely resembling their description. If either was spotted, rotating tails would be set up on the subject—no contact would be made.

As the crowd of departing passengers began to thin, Dixon approached the train's porters, one by one, showing them the pictures. No one recalled having seen the two passengers.

"You are just a few meters from the phones," said Rousseau's techie who was on the phone with Dixon. "I'm calling both numbers now."

A second or two later, Dixon heard the ring tones of two cell phones just behind him. He turned, saw no one, and began rummaging around the seats.

"I've got the phones," said Dixon. "They were left on the train as instructed."

"And the two subjects?" asked Rousseau's man.

"No sign of them yet," Dixon reported. Maybe Churchill was right. "We're going to keep looking," he added. "They might still be here."

Armstrong and Prescott were wrapping things up at the Old Star Pub when Prescott said something that gave his partner pause.

"Eddie . . . how does this end?"

Armstrong took off his coat, hung it back on the rack beside his table, and pulled out his cell phone.

"Hi, hon . . . no, I'm running a little late . . . no, but I'm not that hungry . . . I'll grab something on the way home . . . no, don't wait up, I might be a while . . . yes, hon . . . yes, hon . . . yes, hon . . . I will . . .I love you too."

Prescott leered at Armstrong.

"What do you know, you're not married," Armstrong responded.

"So, how's this going to end?" Armstrong restated the question on the table. "Well, for some it has already ended quite badly," he noted. "The Franklins, Ryan Wright, Constable Jackson—and I'm afraid there's a lot of ugly still ahead of us."

"We can't let Olivia Franklin be touched," said Prescott. "Too high a price has already been paid."

"And we can't bring Churchill, Dixon, and whoever else is involved to any kind of traditional justice. This can never go public, never go to trial, never be known to all but a select few," Armstrong said.

"Well, so far the explosion was reported in the press—then reported again as an IRA plot—then reported a third time when we quashed that story with Ripley's retraction of the bombing theory. So far, that's holding," said Prescott. "Of course everyone at the hospital knows that Olivia was attacked and then disappeared, but the press never got hold of that."

"Thank god," said Armstrong. "The business at Gatwick and Saint Pancras was brushed aside as a training mission, and the deaths of Wright and Jackson have been kept under wraps."

"Okay, so we've been lucky so far, but that's not going to last," said Prescott. "There is only so long that we can contain this before it breaks wide open. You know it, and I know it."

There was silence for a moment, and then Prescott said, "Maybe Olivia needs to go public. Hold a press conference, telling the world who she is."

"That would certainly break things open," said Armstrong. "Any investigative journalist worth his salt would connect the dots, raising more questions than answers and drawing the Royal Family right into the heart of this. No. That's no good. Besides, I don't know if Olivia wants the world to know about this."

"Do you think if Churchill believed that Olivia didn't want any of that, he will let it go?"

"No, I do not think that, and even if it's a possibility, can we really afford to take that chance?" said Armstrong.

"So, the way this ends is either with Olivia being eliminated or with Churchill and his crew being taken out," said Prescott. "And since the only way of ensuring Olivia's survival is to neutralize Churchill and his boys, this becomes a seek-and-destroy mission for you and me," said Prescott, pounding his fist on the table. "Well that is not what I signed up for," he said angrily. "I did not become a policeman to end up as an assassin working outside the law."

The two men just stared at each other. Finally Armstrong spoke.

"Barmaid," he shouted to a pretty girl who was serving nearby tables. "Two Scotch whiskeys, please."

Churchill was driving around Paris, scanning the crowds of tourists at all the popular attractions. It was a long shot, to be sure, that he might just happen by chance upon Olivia or Daniel, but he didn't have any other leads at the moment, so why not?

He'd been to the Louvre, the Eiffel Tower, Notre Dame, and the Left Bank. Now, he was driving down the famed Champs-Élysées, which, despite the late hour, was alive with people eating and drinking in the many restaurants and sidewalk cafes.

🐾

"I'm hungry," said Olivia. "Would you care to join me for a late dinner?"

🐾

Churchill decided to park his car and stroll past the restaurants and cafes. He was on the south side of the broad avenue, examining every face. After about a half a mile, he crossed and began walking up the north side. He found his eyes being drawn to every couple, carefully measuring the height of their seated bodies. He looked up for a moment, and about three cafes further up the street, he saw a couple being seated at a small bistro. Her back was to him, and the light didn't give him a good look at the man's face, but it was them. He was sure of it.

A second later his cell rang.

"They're not here," said Dixon. "I found a porter who recognized them from their pictures. He said they got on and off the train in Paris, and never returned. I think they got on just to ditch their phones."

"They're here," said Churchill. "I . . ."

"You're probably right," said Dixon.

"No, I mean, they're right here. Not fifty meters from where I'm standing," Churchill explained.

"My god! What are you going to do?" asked Dixon.

109

Churchill reached into his coat pocket and felt his revolver.

"I'm going to end this now," he answered, and ended the call.

He walked slowly toward the table where they were seated. He knew that shooting them in public meant a run for his life, but at least the matter would be settled.

"No worries," he said to himself, pulling back the trigger of his gun.

It was at that very moment that the room service waiter knocked on Daniel and Olivia's door.

Dixon was back at the airport when his cell rang.

"What happened?" he asked, when he recognized the caller.

"False alarm," Churchill answered. "A very attractive Swedish couple who very nearly got their brains blown out."

"So, what now?" asked Dixon.

"I want a meeting in the morning with you and Rousseau. We need a better plan."

Chapter Seventeen

Daniel and Olivia awoke to another spring-like day with mild temperatures and lots of sunshine. They had decided to take in some of the sights of Paris, beginning with the Cathedral at Notre Dame.

"I can't really explain it," said Olivia of her choice of Paris attractions. "I think that as a Protestant, I've always had a special interest in Catholicism. Don't forget, all four of my parents were Protestants. Don't you think that most Protestants have an inborn fascination with the Catholic Church? I mean, were it not for Henry the Eighth, we'd all be Catholics."

"I suppose," said Daniel. "I'm much more interested in the Church's art and architecture."

"Well, that too," said Olivia, filling a small day pack that she had purchased the day before. "Shall I bring my laptop?" she asked Daniel.

"Bring your iPad. We haven't had a chance to check that out yet."

"When's our next contact with Armstrong?" she asked.

"No set time," he answered. "But, if ever there was a case of 'no news is good news,' this would be it."

"Do you think Churchill may have given up?" she asked him.

"I think that until we hear otherwise, we should assume that Mr. Churchill is ten meters behind us and ready to pounce."

"Well, that's reassuring," Olivia said sarcastically.

"I don't say it to be reassuring, sweetheart." Daniel walked over to her and took her hands. "You are the most precious thing in the world to me. I take your safety and well-being quite seriously."

They exchanged a quick kiss, grabbed their packs, and headed out.

Armstrong and Prescott were huddled over the coffee pot down the hall from Armstrong's office when Smitty turned the corner.

"Gentlemen," he said, upon seeing them. "I believe I have some information you may be interested in."

The three men walked to Armstrong's office and made themselves comfortable.

"So, what have you got, Smitty?" Armstrong asked.

"Your search parameters were spot on," he began. "I've got the full monty for you."

"Let's hear it," said Prescott.

Smitty opened a file and started to read.

"Eduard Rousseau joined the Sûreté in 1964 and was rapidly promoted, ultimately attaining the rank of Brigadier-Major. He first crossed paths with RMP Major Hugh Dixon in the summer of 1967."

"And just how did that come about?" asked Armstrong.

"It's an interesting story," Smitty continued. "In 1967, the Canadians put on a World's Fair, of sorts, calling it Expo '67."

"I remember that," said Armstrong. "It came on the heels of the New York World's Fair. Wasn't there some sort of political controversy swirling around that event?"

"There was, indeed," said Smitty. "Throughout the mid '60s there was a growing movement by the French Canadians in the eastern part of the country to separate from the rest of Canada and become an independent country. The heart of that movement was in French-speaking Montreal, where the Exposition was held."

"As I recall," said Prescott, jumping in, "the Queen was none too keen on all of that."

"That would be something of an understatement," said Armstrong budding in. "It's all coming back to me now. It was all over the news, and it created quite a bit of tension between the UK and France."

"France?" said Prescott. "Why France?"

"In a word?" said Smitty. "De Gaulle."

"Now I remember," said Armstrong. "This was near the end of Charles de Gaulle's presidency. He was losing popularity with his people, and in a bid to rekindle French nationalism, he became quite outspoken about the French Canadian Separatist movement. This did not sit well with Her Majesty, who never was all that fond of de Gaulle in the first place."

"Great, but what does that have to do with Dixon and Rousseau?" said Prescott, who was growing impatient.

Armstrong turned to Smitty, who continued with his briefing.

"I'm afraid it has everything to do with Rousseau and Dixon," Smitty explained. "You see, in July of 1967, de Gaulle announced that he would visit the Canadian Exposition. This made the Queen livid because, knowing de Gaulle as she did, she knew that the sole purpose of the visit was to stir up the separatists. This was tantamount to challenging the Queen's sovereignty over a Commonwealth nation—something she would have none of."

"The result," Smitty continued, "was that she insisted on having her own people on the ground for the French president's visit, a contingent that included a number of RMPs, including Dixon."

"And that's when Dixon met Rousseau?" asked Prescott.

"Not just met him," Smitty went on. "The two of them were teamed up for the event, and they became fast friends from the get-go."

"Define friends," said Armstrong.

"Buddies, pals, chums, mates," said Smitty. "Their families have vacationed together; Dixon introduced Rousseau to the game of golf; Rousseau attended Dixon's daughter's wedding; since Dixon's retirement and Rousseau's semi-retirement, they've seen even more of one another."

"What do you mean, Rousseau's semi-retirement?" Prescott asked.

"When he left the Sûreté, he started a private investigative firm that has grown to be quite successful. They are headquartered in Paris, and they seem to be rather tech- smart."

Smitty held up a small electronic device that no one recognized. "The tap on Tom and Helen Franklin's phone," he explained.

"Smitty, I need you to put that back on that line," Armstrong said quickly.

"Already have," said Smitty with a smile. "Slightly modified so we can listen and trace, as well."

"Good job, Smitty." said Armstrong. "Keep me in the loop on this one."

"Will do," said Smitty, who stood and left the room.

"So, what do you think?" asked Prescott.

"Well, there's no guarantee that this Rousseau chap is involved with Churchill and Dixon, but that's where I'd put my money," said Armstrong.

"How do we confirm . . . no, wait," he said suddenly realizing. "Smitty's tap will take care of that."

Armstrong just smiled.

Rousseau's techie in London walked out of the Apple store on Regent Street, looking quite satisfied. He pulled out his cell and called Rousseau at his office in Paris.

"I think we hit the mother lode," said the techie. "Sim card numbers, GPS tracking info, serial numbers, cookies—everything we should need to locate them."

"I want you back in this office before noon," Rousseau instructed his employee before ending the call.

"Good news, I hope?" said Dixon, who was sitting in a high-backed armchair facing Rousseau's desk.

"We could use some," added Churchill who sat in an identical chair in a position adjacent to Dixon's.

"My man in London located the store where they purchased all their phones and computer gear. We should have everything we need to find them in a couple of hours."

"That is good news," said Dixon. "The girl's parents are very worried about her," he said to Rousseau, while glancing at Churchill.

Daniel and Olivia took the Paris Metro to Notre Dame. Taking the Metro is as much a tourist activity in Paris as visiting Montmartre or taking a boat tour of the Seine. It's the kind of thing that makes you feel a little bit Parisian.

Emerging from the Metro, Daniel and Olivia beheld the western façade of Notre Dame de Paris, which translates in English to *Our Lady of Paris*. One of the finest examples of French Gothic architecture, construction began in 1163, and many Parisians joke that it will really be something when it's finished.

Despite the scaffolding that seems to be a permanent fixture for cleaning and repairs, the grand dame is awe-inspiring from any angle. Though there was extensive vandalism during the French Revolution, the cathedral today is regarded by many as the most glorious outside the Vatican.

They were just about to enter the great church when Daniel's pre-paid cell rang.

"Good morning," he said to Armstrong.

"Good morning," said Armstrong. "How are you two doing?"

"Okay," said Daniel. "We seem to be managing a constant nervousness that keeps us alert but allows us to function. What can you tell us?" he asked.

"Put Olivia on," he answered.

"He wants to talk to you," Daniel said to Olivia, handing her the phone.

"Hello," she said.

"Good morning, Olivia. How are you holding up?" Armstrong asked.

"Pretty good," she answered. "This whole business is more than a bit surreal. Do you know where Churchill is?" she asked him.

"We think so," he answered. "We need your help to confirm it. Here's what I'd like you to do."

In a room full of computers and wide array of technical gear, Rousseau, Dixon, Churchill, and Rousseau's head of technical surveillance, Jacque Marquand, were huddled around a speaker listening to a conversation between Olivia and her Aunt Helen. Olivia's voice was raspy and weak, as though she had a bad case of laryngitis.

"I'm fine, Aunt Helen. Really," said Olivia in almost a whisper.

"You don't sound fine," said her aunt. "You don't even sound like you."

"I know. I have a nasty cold," said Olivia. "I always seem to get sick when I visit France."

"You're in France?" said Helen, sounding rather surprised.

"Yes, but just for a few more hours. I'm driving to Switzerland this afternoon. I'll call you from there, okay?"

"Please do, Liv. Your uncle and I are so worried about you," said Helen.

"I have to go now, Aunt Helen. I'll talk to you later. Goodbye."

"What can you tell us, Jacque?" Rousseau asked Marquand.

"The call originated from a cell near Notre Dame. It's definitely one of the phones they purchased at the Apple store."

"Buggers!" said Churchill. "That may have been the girl's phone, but that wasn't Olivia Franklin."

"Why do you say that?" asked Dixon.

"In the first place, it didn't sound anything like Olivia Franklin," said Churchill. "Besides, do you really think she would tell her aunt that she's in France? No, this is another red herring. Armstrong got somebody to make that call to throw us off. My guess is that Armstrong found the tap on her aunt and uncle's phone, and they concocted this ruse to make us think she's in Paris."

"Well, if she's not in Paris, we have nothing to go on," said Rousseau. "I suggest we go to Notre Dame without delay."

"I'm telling you, it's a waste of time," said Churchill, appearing quite dejected.

And then they all got up and left.

"Number 17 Quay d'Orsay," said Smitty to Armstrong and Prescott. "The call was traced to the offices of Rousseau's investigative agency."

Armstrong turned to Prescott.

"Is your passport up to date?" he asked him.

Chapter Eighteen

As Rousseau, Dixon, Churchill, and several of Rousseau's operatives were scouring Notre Dame and its environs, Daniel and Olivia were headed back to their hotel. Despite the pictures being shown to tourists and docents, inside and outside Notre Dame, no one recalled seeing Daniel or Olivia; with every passing minute, Churchill was growing deeper in his conviction that the two had never been there and that someone else had made that call.

When Armstrong and Prescott pulled up to Armstrong's home so he could pack a bag for their trip to Paris, neither man noticed the blue Volvo that had followed them from Scotland Yard. It parked down the street about a hundred meters from the small row house—behind its tinted windows; the driver was focused on their every move.

In his quarters in the palace, His Royal Highness was anxious that he hadn't heard from Churchill. This whole affair was taking too long, with too many loose ends. He couldn't help wondering if the very scandal he'd hoped to stave off would explode in his face, making an even greater mess than originally anticipated.

✦

"Do you get the feeling that no matter what is being played out between Armstrong and Churchill we'd be better off getting out of Paris?" Daniel asked Olivia as they emerged from the Metro and began the short walk to their hotel.

"I don't know what to think," she answered. "Your friend, Eddie, has taken pretty good care of us so far."

"Yes, Eddie's the best," he answered. "But, I just don't feel like we are masters of our own fate. That business back at the Cathedral was like a game—like the phones on the train to Barcelona. It all makes me very nervous."

"So, why don't we just get as far away from here as we can, and not tell anyone," suggested Olivia.

"I think I'd feel less nervous," said Daniel.

"So, let's do it," said Olivia. "We'll go the hotel and gather our belongings and take off."

She took his hand, and the two of them just walked. They were about two blocks from their hotel off the Champs-Élysées when the sound of screeching tires caught their attention, turning their heads just in time to see a red Peugeot slam into a young boy on a bicycle. In an instant, Olivia was off the curb and into the street, racing toward the boy.

"Olivia!" Daniel shouted, chasing after her.

By the time Daniel got there, Olivia was checking the boy's vital signs. He was unconscious and his breathing was shallow, but he was alive. One look, and Daniel could see that the boy's left leg was badly mangled. A growing red stain on the boy's pant leg was of greater concern.

"Let me in there," Daniel said to Olivia, withdrawing a pocketknife from his jeans. He quickly cut away the boys pants so as to view the wound.

Daniel and Olivia just looked at each other—no need for words. The boy's femur was badly broken and the femoral artery was lacerated and squirting blood. Daniel applied pressure, while Olivia jumped up and began addressing the gathering crowd.

"We are doctors," she said in English. For those who didn't understand, others were quickly translating. "This boy has been seriously injured. If we don't treat him now, he will be dead in three minutes."

"Show them Daniel," she said to him. Daniel released his thumb, and the crowd watched in horror as blood spurt high into the air. The crowd gasped.

"We need your help," said Olivia to the growing crowd. "We have to do surgery right here and now. We need bandages, knives, alcohol, belts—look through your purses and packages to see what you have."

Many in the crowd were carrying shopping bags. Others looked in their handbags, while one man removed his belt and handed it to Olivia.

"You speak English?" she asked him.

"A little," he responded.

"Get us what we need," she instructed. "I have to help my partner."

Olivia crouched down to lend Daniel a hand. She immediately applied the man's belt to the upper part of the boy's thigh, pulling the belt as hard as she could to use it as a tourniquet.

"I'm going to have to get in there for a closer look," Daniel said without looking up. A tap on Olivia's shoulder turned her around to see the man she had spoken with holding a bottle of vodka and some newly purchased white linen shirts.

"Tear the shirts into strips," she said to the man and those beside him. Olivia grabbed the Vodka and poured some on Daniel's hands and over the wound.

A woman in the crowd who saw Daniel struggling to make an incision in the boy's leg pulled out a set of brand new steak knives and handed them to Olivia. A moment later, the knife was sterilized with vodka and in Daniel's confident hands. The crowd leaned and watched as Daniel enlarged the incision. Without a word spoken, Olivia grabbed one of the white shirts, not yet torn, and used it to mop up the blood so Daniel could see what he was doing.

"I need clamps," he shouted as he exposed the torn artery.

"Clamps," shouted Olivia, jumping to her feet. The man who had given her the belt was trying to translate. "Hair clips, paper clips, anything we can use to clamp the arteries."

An elderly man offered the top of his ballpoint pen. It had a clip on it.

"Yes," Olivia shouted, dousing it in alcohol and handing it to Daniel. "More. We need more," Olivia said to the crowd.

As Olivia bent back down to apply a tourniquet to the lower part of the boy's leg, an assortment of clips of various sorts were being sterilized with vodka by one of the women, who offered them to Daniel on pieces of alcohol-soaked cloth.

"I've almost got it," said Daniel, his fingers deep into the boy's leg. "How's his pulse?"

Olivia checked for a pulse in the boy's neck.

"I'm not getting anything," she told Daniel. "I think he's stopped breathing."

"I'm almost there," Daniel answered. "Start CPR."

The crowd held its breath as Olivia clamped the boy's nose with her fingers, tilted back his head, and began breathing into his mouth. After only a few breaths, the boy let out a moan and opened his eyes.

An audible gasp went up from the crowd as the boy started crying and grasping his leg.

As sirens could be heard approaching from some distance, Daniel tied off some bandages to bind the wound, while Olivia comforted the boy.

"It's okay," she said. "You're going to be okay."

Suddenly the crowd erupted into applause.

Daniel, looking up for the first time, saw dozens of people taking pictures on their cell phones. A couple of tourists were capturing the action on video cameras.

As the sirens grew louder, Daniel grabbed Olivia's hand.

"We have to go," he said to her.

"We can't just leave him," Olivia answered.

Ambulances and police cars could be seen rounding the corner.

Tugging on her arm, Daniel yanked her up off the ground, took her by her shoulders, and said in a most urgent tone, "Now! We've got to get out of here now!"

Olivia understood, and the two turned and ran.

Chapter Nineteen

Daniel and Olivia ran the two blocks to their hotel, loped up the stairs to their room and started packing.

"Where are we going?" Olivia asked him.

"I don't know, but we need to get there quickly," Daniel answered.

"Are we leaving Paris?" she asked.

"A soon as we possibly can. We are going to be all over the news in a couple of hours."

It dawned on Olivia that Daniel was almost certainly correct. They had just performed surgery in the middle of the Champs-Élysées in front of dozens of witnesses, most of whom had cameras. Packing her laptop, she couldn't help thinking that nowadays every person with a decent cell phone was a photojournalist.

"How are we going to get out of the city?" she asked him as she gathered her clothes.

"We need a car, and we need it fast," he answered.

"So we rent a car and go," she said calmly.

"I don't think it's going to be that easy," Daniel said as he was stuffing his belongings into a nylon duffle. "That phone call you made to your aunt and uncle . . . I think that was meant to fool Churchill into thinking that we are not in Paris."

"So?"

"So, if it didn't fool him, we have to assume that he and whoever may be helping him has every exit covered, including rental car agencies," Daniel answered.

"Do you really think that's possible?" Olivia asked him.

"Do you really want to chance that?" he replied.

Daniel looked at Olivia, who was zipping up her bag, stepped forward and gave her a hard kiss. "Let's go," he said, taking her hand and leading her out of the room.

⁕

In the British Airways terminal at Heathrow, Armstrong and Prescott had completed check-in and were waiting at the gate for their flight to board. They had checked one bag, which would add to the time it would take to get into the city, but it was the only way to bring firearms into France. Though they were permitted to carry their service weapons throughout Europe, they could not be worn or taken as carry-on luggage on a plane, a small price to pay for keeping air travel safe. Wouldn't want some maniac grabbing your gun as you're trying to squeeze past the beverage cart to use the head.

As they sat in the lounge, Armstrong wrote a note on a card he had bought at the gift shop. The message was short and to the point:

Phillip Churchill and Hugh Dixon must be stopped before this whole business spins out of control.

Respectfully,

Chief Inspector Edward Armstrong, Metropolitan Police Service

"I'm just going to post this," he said to Prescott as he was addressing the envelope.

126

Armstrong rose and walked to a nearby post box. Before dropping it in, he looked at the envelope and shuddered. The card was addressed to:

Her Majesty, Queen Elizabeth II
Buckingham Palace
London SW1A 1AA

In Rousseau's office in Paris, Dixon and Churchill sat in the tech suite listening to a recording of the phone call made by Olivia Franklin earlier in the day.

"Christ, Phillip. We've listened to this thing twenty times. What do you expect to find?" said Dixon.

Churchill just ignored him, turned to the tech wizard, Marquand, and asked, "What time was this call made?"

"Around 11:00 a.m," Marquand answered.

Churchill flew out of his chair and grabbed Marquand by the shoulders.

"Not around what time," he shouted, spraying the man's face. "WHAT TIME?"

Marquand tapped on the keyboard of his computer and in less than five seconds said, "10:59:07 to 10:59:58."

"Play it again," said Churchill. "Only this time, let it keep playing after the girl says goodbye."

They listened to the phone call, yet again, only this time Marquand let it keep playing.

"There," Churchill said excitedly. "At the very end—what's that sound?"

Marquand replayed the last few seconds of the tape, pushing the volume to reveal an odd clank.

"That," said Churchill. "What is that?"

Marquand put on a pair of headphones, tapped a bunch of commands into his computer, and replayed the clank.

He then spun in his chair, and said to Churchill, "That, Sir, is a fragment of the first strike of a church bell chiming the hour."

"Blimey!" said Dixon. "They were at Notre Dame."

Churchill stared eerily at nothing.

"They're here," he said softly.

Daniel and Olivia didn't bother to check out of their hotel. They simply dashed past the desk clerk and onto the street, where they flagged the first taxi that came by.

"Place Vendôme," Daniel shouted, as he and Olivia climbed into the taxi.

"So, what's the plan, love?" Olivia said smoothly.

Daniel explained that Place Vendôme was a broad square just past the Élysée Palace, virtually surrounded by hotels.

"My hope is that we can get the concierge at one of those hotels to have a rental car delivered to us, so we can avoid going to an agency," Daniel explained.

"Do hotels do that sort of thing?" Olivia asked.

"We're about to find out," said Daniel.

"And if we are so fortunate as to get out of Paris, then what?" she asked him.

"I don't know," he answered. "Think about where you'd like to go," he said.

"Hmmm," said Olivia. "Do you surf?"

As they approached the Place Vendôme, which was all of a five-minute ride from their last hotel, the driver asked where they would like to be let off. Daniel and Olivia just looked at each other.

"This is good," said Olivia. "I need to stretch my legs," she said to Daniel with a devilish smirk.

They stepped from the taxi and looked around.

Place Vendôme is a square mile in area, with a huge column at the center of the square that was originally erected by Napoleon. Repeatedly torn down and reconstructed over the centuries, the Place Vendôme Column is widely considered to be the least artistic column in the world, and its latest erection appears to be just that—a giant phallic symbol that celebrates nothing beyond Napoleon's grandiose sense of self.

As Daniel and Olivia gazed around the square, they saw dozens of hotels, each more opulent than the last.

"Where shall we begin?" asked Olivia.

"Let's try that one," Daniel answered, pointing to the Park Hyatt, which he knew to be one of the more luxurious Hotels in Paris.

"Why that one?" she asked.

"It's American owned," Daniel answered. "In France, be it McDonald's, Disneyland, or hotels, the Americans always seem to try a little too hard."

ﾉﾊﾊ

On the flight from London to Paris, Armstrong and Prescott were discussing their course of action.

"Either way, the key is to take Rousseau out of the picture," said Prescott. "Without his agency's resources, Churchill and Dixon will be flying blind."

"Please don't speak of flying blind while we're in the air," said Armstrong. "But you're right," he continued. "Rousseau is the key. The question is, how much does he know about what's really going on, and is he willing to jeopardize his agency and his future by engaging in a criminal conspiracy?"

"And how do you propose we answer those questions?" Prescott asked.

"I say we put it to him directly, outside the presence of Churchill and Dixon, as soon as possible," said Armstrong. "Oh, and one more thing."

"What's that?" said Prescott.

"Are you going to eat those pretzels?"

🐾

At the Hôtel du Rond-Point, the day shift desk clerk was getting ready to leave when a report on the television caught his eye. It was all about two doctors, a man and women, both reported to be British, who had saved the life of nine year-old Jean-Paul León, son of the shipping magnate Henri León. The pictures of the two doctors were, of course, familiar to the clerk, who watched in amazement as the TV rolled video of the doctors performing surgery right in the middle of the Champs-Élysées.

"I just want to thank these people who saved my son's life," said the senior León with tears in his eyes. "If anyone watching knows these brave heroes or how I may contact them, please call this number."

The hotel clerk made a note of the number that appeared at the bottom of the TV screen, and picked up the telephone that sat on his desk.

🐾

In Rousseau's office, Dixon, Churchill, and Rousseau were excitedly watching the same TV news report when the techie Marquand burst into the room.

"They are registered at Hôtel du Rond-Point, just two blocks from where the accident occurred."

Without a word, Dixon and Churchill jumped to their feet and dashed out the door.

🐾

"Oui, Monsieur. We can take you to any of the nearby rental agencies," said the concierge at the Park Hyatt.

"No. You don't understand. I need a rental car brought here," Daniel explained.

"But, Monsieur, it is much faster to let us drive you to the rental place. To have them come to you is something that is not done. It makes no sense."

"Daniel, let's go," said Olivia. "Merci," she said to the concierge, and steered Daniel away.

"Maybe we should just take our chances and go rent a car," she suggested.

Daniel looked flustered.

"Excuse me," said a man of about thirty with a thick cockney accent. "I couldn't help overhearing your conversation with the concierge. I think I can help you."

Daniel eyed the man up and down, paying special attention to the miles of intricate, swirling tattoos on his forearms and his lime green pants below an orange t-shirt and a bright red poplin sports jacket.

"And you are?" Daniel asked him.

The man extended his hand in a friendly greeting. "Nigel Baker," he said with a broad smile. "Road Manager of the Goo-Goos."

Daniel shook the man's hand and returned the smile. "So, how can you help us?" he asked.

"Oh, the only reason the concierge didn't do it for you is because you're not a celebrity," he explained. "Most of the better hotels around here will provide that service if you're Britney Spears or Paris Hilton or the Prime Minister's underage mistress."

Olivia couldn't help laughing, which Nigel didn't seem to mind a bit.

"Come with me," said Nigel, taking her hand. "There's a place down the street which I guarantee will help you with this."

As the three of them moved towards the door to the street, Nigel continued to yammer.

"Here on holiday, are you?" he asked.

"Not exactly," said Olivia. "More of a quick getaway," she told him.

"Ah, a weekend escape," Nigel responded.

"You could say that," said Daniel, who was starting to enjoy the young man. "And this place you're taking us will have a rental car delivered to us?"

"Well, you might have to check in to get that service. Will that be a problem?"

"Not at all," said Olivia. "What is the place, anyway?" she asked.

"The best Paris has to offer," Nigel responded. "There is nothing quite like a stay at the Ritz."

Chapter Twenty

The British Airways flight from London to Paris had just landed, and Armstrong and Prescott were huddled over the baggage carousel to claim their checked luggage.

"I suggest we rent a car and go straight to Rousseau's office," said Armstrong.

"What if Churchill is there? I don't think he'd hesitate to shoot us both," said Prescott.

"No, I don't imagine he would," said Armstrong. "We'll just have to make sure neither he nor Dixon is there when we see Rousseau."

A few moments later, the one piece of checked luggage arrived and the two policemen headed for the rental car counters.

"Here, let me carry that," Prescott said to his partner. "I find it reassuring to be close to my weapon."

Armstrong gave him a knowing glance.

At the Hôtel du Rond-Point, the desk clerk was looking through the hotel register, trying to assist the two Englishmen who were inquiring about the British doctors.

"Oui, Monsieur, they are still checked in but do not appear to be here at the moment."

"Well, where are they?" barked Churchill.

"How would I know that?" replied the clerk, seeming a bit put off.

"You did call in to the Sûreté to report their presence here, did you not?"

"No, Monsieur. I assure you I made no such call," the clerk answered. "Sûreté? What, may I ask, is this about?" said the clerk, somewhat confused.

"You did not make that call after seeing the report on the BBC about the accident?" asked Churchill.

"I'm sorry, Monsieur. I have no idea what you are talking about. Were the doctors in an accident?"

"Christ!" said Churchill, pounding a fist on the counter.

"Come on, Phillip," said Dixon. "We are wasting our time."

"Un moment, Monsieurs," said the clerk. He picked up the phone and dialed a number.

"Paul, il y a deux anglais ici se renseignant sur les docteurs et un accident . . . oui . . . oui . . . ah, oui . . . oui, oui, oui. Merci, Paul."

"Ah, gentleman," he said to Churchill and Dixon. "Pardon. It was Paul, the daytime desk clerk who saw it on the TV and made the call. There is some kind of reward, no?"

"Yes, I believe there is," said Dixon.

"Did your friend, Paul, say when the doctors would be back?" asked Churchill.

"No, I'm afraid not," said the clerk. "But he did say that when they got into the taxi, he heard the man tell the driver to take them to Place Vendôme."

Churchill and Dixon quickly turned and headed for the door.

"I will share in reward?" the clerk yelled after them.

He got no response.

While Prescott drove the Avis rental, Armstrong punched in the number of Rousseau's investigative agency.

"Yes, this is Mr. Quinn in London. I am an associate of Mr. Phillip Churchill. He left this number in case I needed to reach him in an emergency. Is he there? It's urgent that I speak with him."

A secretary told Armstrong that Churchill and his friend had left the office about thirty minutes prior. She didn't know when they would be back, and asked if he'd like to leave a message or speak with Mr. Rousseau.

"Yes," he told her. "Would you ask Mr. Churchill to call Quinn in London? He has the number . . . Merci," said Armstrong.

"I didn't know you spoke French," Prescott quipped.

"Well, now you've heard the lot of it," he answered.

"Churchill and Dixon aren't there," Armstrong went on. "But Rousseau apparently is, and I suggest we move it."

Prescott stomped on the accelerator and weaved the car through the late-day traffic.

It cost Daniel and Olivia nearly 500 euro to check in to the Ritz for one night—not a usurious amount, if they had been planning to actually stay there.

Nigel had already arranged for the rental car to be delivered and put on Daniel's bill. There would be no papers for Daniel to sign, no license to show; the hotel would take care of all of that. The concierge didn't even bat an eye when he was told that the couple was travelling incognito—too high profile to even have their real names mentioned—there are people in this world who, by wealth, celebrity or political power, play by an entirely different set of rules.

"Your car will be here in about twenty minutes," Nigel informed them. "I assume a Mercedes will be adequate."

Olivia turned and walked across the lobby, sitting herself down in an overstuffed armchair.

"Is she alright?" Nigel asked Daniel.

"It's kind of hard to explain," Daniel replied.

Changing the subject, Daniel extended his hand and said, "Nigel, you have no idea how much you've helped us today. We really do appreciate it."

Daniel reached into his pocket and pulled out a roll of British pounds.

"Don't even think about it, mate," said Nigel backing off a step.

"Thank you, Nigel. We do appreciate it." Daniel started to turn when the young Englishman asked him a question.

"Hey! Anybody ever tell you that your lady looks just like Princess Di?"

"We get a lot of that," said Daniel, before pivoting and walking to Olivia.

"Are you okay?" he asked her, knowing she was not.

"Oh, sure, I'm just peachy," she responded. "I'm sitting in the hotel where my biological mother Diana was last seen smiling. I'm about to get into the same kind of car in which took her last breaths. What's next, paparazzi chasing us out of the hotel?"

Daniel crouched down in front of her and took her hands in hers.

"I have to admit, it's a bit spooky," Daniel said. "But this is an entirely different situation. The only people looking for you have no idea where you are; and besides . . ."

"You're here with me," she said. "And I have never felt as completely safe as when I'm with you."

"Remember that," he said to her, leaning in for a kiss. "We are okay, and we always will be, as long as we're together."

✸

Churchill and Dixon jumped out of their Europcar rental and did a slow, 360 degree reconnoiter of their surroundings.

136

"Jesus! This place is huge," said Dixon. "I sure hope you've got a plan that's better than mine."

"What's yours?" asked Churchill.

"Walk around until we bump into them?"

Churchill pulled out his phone and punched in the numbers for Rousseau. Inside Rousseau's office, the retired Sûreté officer turned to Armstrong.

"It's Churchill," said Rousseau to the men from Scotland Yard.

"Take the call," said Armstrong.

Rousseau answered his phone, saying, "Yes?"

"Have you got anything new for us?" Churchill asked him.

Rousseau stared at Armstrong and Prescott for a moment.

"No. Nothing," he said to Churchill. "No phone calls or computer use. No sightings. Where are you?" asked Rousseau.

"Place Vendôme," Churchill answered. "They came here by taxi not an hour ago."

"Okay. I'll send some of my people," said Rousseau before hitting end on his cell.

Rousseau leaned back in his desk chair and regarded Armstrong and Prescott.

"Listen. Like I said, none of what you've told me is anything like what I've been led to believe," Rousseau told the two detectives. "Hugh called me a couple of days ago and asked me to help him locate the daughter of a client of his. He said there was a big reward. He also said that Churchill is a longtime friend of his, as Dixon is of mine. But those pictures of the dead policemen, and that call I made earlier to my men in London, tell a different story. The thing is..." Rousseau paused for a long few seconds. "... I cannot give up these men to you. Do you understand?"

"I believe I do," said Armstrong. Prescott nodded agreement.

"You didn't know what you were getting yourself into," said Prescott. "You were just trying to help out a good friend. I understand. Dixon may be doing the same thing for his old friend, without knowing the whole story."

"The question is," Armstrong cut in. "What are you going to do now?"

Rousseau thought for a moment then rose from his chair.

"Monsieurs," he began. "There is a lovely, much too young lady meeting me at my home at 7:00 p.m. If you don't mind, I'm calling it a day."

Armstrong looked at Prescott, and the two of them stood up and followed Rousseau out of the office.

After bidding Rousseau "bon soir" as he strode off down the street, Prescott turned to Armstrong and said, "So, what do you think, Eddie?"

"I believe him," said Armstrong. "But, we shall see what we shall see."

※

"Monsieur," said the Ritz Hotel concierge to Daniel. "Your car has arrived. This way, please."

Daniel and Olivia looked at one another and proceeded to follow the officious Frenchman toward the entrance.

※

"We're close. I know we are," said Churchill to Dixon as they walked down the Rue de la Paix toward the grandest hotels on Place Vendôme.

Just at that moment, Daniel and Olivia exited the Ritz and walked to the awaiting Mercedes Benz with the rental car agent standing beside the open driver's side door. Not a heartbeat later, the two spotted Churchill and Dixon, who saw them as well. Olivia would later say that it was a moment that felt like an hour as the four of them just stared at each other.

Chapter Twenty-One

"It's them," yelled Churchill, taking off toward the entrance to the Ritz. "Get the car," he shouted at the top of his lungs.

Daniel turned to the rental agent and said, "Meet us around back." Then he quickly grabbed Olivia's arm and jerked her back into the hotel. They sprinted hand-in-hand down the grand center hall that ran the length of the hotel from the Place de Vendôme entrance to the smaller Rue Cambon entrance. With every step, they drew stares from hotel guests and staff, unsure of what they were seeing. Olivia was equally unsure about what was going on.

The Mercedes was already there when they exited the building, and they quickly got in. Daniel took the wheel and, in a screech of spinning wheels, left ribbons of tire marks as he floored the Mercedes down Rue Cambon toward the Place de la Concorde.

"Tell me this isn't happening," screamed Olivia to Daniel. She was fully aware that they had just left the Ritz in precisely the same manner as her mother Diana, almost fourteen years earlier—the very night she had died. Pursued, as she had been, by relentless men with their own cruel agenda, it felt almost dreamlike as they raced down the narrow street.

"Stay to the right!" she shouted, as an oncoming car seemed headed for the bridge of her nose. We are not in the UK stay on the right side of the road, Darling."

Twisting in her seat to peer out the rear window, she saw no other cars. And then she did—a gray Citroen sliding around a corner, two blocks back.

"Shit!" she said, pounding on the dashboard. "They're behind us, Daniel! They're chasing us, Daniel!"

Daniel made a left, a right, a left, and another right, and tore down Rue de Rivoli. Olivia closed her eyes and tried to go to a quiet place.

In a blink, she was transported across space and time to her childhood home in Knightsbridge. She was a gangly sixteen year-old, stretched out on a couch in her parents' front room, watching late night television. It was well past midnight, and she very much enjoyed the old Monty Python reruns, which she thought were brilliant.

Abruptly, the TV screen was overtaken by a BBC Breaking News graphic and a newscaster reporting that Princess Diana had been in a car accident in Paris. There were few details at the time, as police, rescue crews, and the TV News had just arrived at the scene—a tunnel somewhere in Paris.

Olivia was entranced by the flickering images in the darkness of the parlor.

Like many British girls, Olivia saw the Princess as a larger than life figure—beautiful, vulnerable, committed to children the world over, a tragic victim of a loveless marriage, spectacular in her grace. And then there was that smile—Olivia's smile, so many had said. It had always made her feel somehow connected to Diana—that night, this moment—always.

Within minutes of the program being interrupted, they were reporting that the accident was serious and that there had been multiple injuries to the passengers in the car. Minutes later there were pictures of a badly crushed and mangled black Mercedes, and the newscaster was reporting that Diana's companion, Dodi Fayed, and the driver of the vehicle, Henri Paul, had been pronounced dead at the scene. The bodyguard was the only survivor.

"Oh, My god!" Olivia said to the darkness.

A minute later her spirits soared when it was announced that Diana had survived the accident and was suffering from a broken arm, a concussion, and lacerations to her thigh, but she was OK and being taken to hospital by ambulance.

"Thank god!" Olivia shouted to the television. "Thank you, god."

Olivia watched the chilling coverage deep into the night. There were reports that the car had been involved in a high-speed chase with paparazzi, conflicting reports that Diana's condition was serious but not life threatening, then critical and very grave. Olivia felt like she was witnessing the most important event of her life.

And then, the BBC reported an unconfirmed statement by the British Press Association that the Princess had died of her injuries. Two minutes later, an announcement from Buckingham Palace confirmed that report.

Olivia was in shock, tears streaming down her face, and then she was jolted again as the Mercedes Daniel was driving hit a curb while making a turn onto Rue de Mondovi.

"Daniel, where are we?" she asked in a voice choked by tears.

"I'm trying to find a motorway," he answered. "We need to get on a road where we can get up some real speed."

Olivia trembled in horror.

�☈

"Stay with him," said Churchill to Dixon who was driving the Citroen. "I'm going to get us some help," he said, taking out his cell phone.

"Rousseau . . . we're following them around the Place de la Concorde. I don't think they know the city because they are making so many lefts and rights that they've hardly gone anywhere . . . if I had another car or two and we could box them in . . . will do."

"What?" said Dixon.

"He's on it. He said to call back in five."

☗37☈

141

Armstrong and Prescott were driving slowly down Place des Pyramides past the beautiful national gardens, Jardin des Tuilereis.

"Do you have a destination in mind, or should I just drive around?" asked Prescott.

"Hold on. I'll find out," said Armstrong. He took out his cell phone and punched in Daniel's number, and as he was about to hit "send," the phone rang.

"It's Rousseau," came the voice on the other end. "I'm not sure why I'm doing this, but I thought I should tell you that Dixon and Churchill are chasing your friends around the Place de la Concorde."

"Thanks," said Armstrong before ending the call and punching in Olivia's number.

When her phone rang, Olivia momentarily jumped out of her seat, but after a couple of deep breaths, the melodic ringtone seemed to have a settling effect that brought her to a more relaxed reality.

"Bon jour," she said cutely. " Paris Tours. Oh, Eddie, thank god . . . well, he's a bit busy at the moment trying to elude the killers that are chasing us . . . can I take a message? . . . Yes . . . yes . . . uh-huh . . . yes . . . yes . . . okay, Eddie. I'll tell him. Bye."

Olivia hit "end" and dropped the phone in her lap.

"Well, what did he say?" Daniel asked her.

"He said remember to stay to the right," she said with a smile that Daniel took to mean, 'we are okay, and we will be.

As Daniel screeched around corners like a movie stunt driver, all became quiet for Olivia, who inexplicably found an unusual degree of serenity. She leaned back in her seat and closed her eyes.

I am Dr. Olivia Franklin. Strong, smart, determined.

I am the grown child of Arthur and Elizabeth Franklin, my loving parents who shaped me into the woman I've become.

I am Princess Diana's biological daughter, the child she never knew.

I am a princess in my own right because I sit beside a prince of a man who is my partner, my lover, my protector, and my friend.

I am a princess of another sort, with a family I have never met—brothers I may never know.

***No, Olivia!** You will not allow that to happen. God, or destiny, or the stars, or a royal ghost have put you here to survive and thrive and to find your brothers to give them a small vestige of their mother.*

Olivia's peace was pure and perfect and punctuated by a bullet shattering the back window of the Mercedes.

"Holy tomtit on a stick!" she shouted. "Daniel. Get us out of here!"

Prescott made a right and another right, heading west on Voie Georges Pompidou. "How are we ever going to find them in all this traffic?" asked Prescott. Just at that moment, he had to slam on the brakes to avoid a black Mercedes and a gray Citroen that came slip sliding around a corner into his path.

"Follow that Citroen," said Armstrong.

The three cars accelerated onto Cours La Reine, an open straightaway that runs along the north bank of the Seine. Within seconds, the powerful Mercedes opened a considerable lead over the other two cars.

Leaning out the passenger side window, Churchill fired several shots at the Mercedes, two of which hit the boot of the car. A moment later, Armstrong leaned out his window and fired one shot through the center of the rear window of the Citroen.

"Buggers!" said Churchill, who had a clear view of Armstrong and Prescott.

Neither Churchill nor Armstrong noticed a fourth car closing in behind them.

As the roadway changed its name from Cours La Reine to Cours Albert, Olivia suddenly realized where they were.

"Oh, my God!" she exclaimed. "The tunnel!"

"Yes, I saw the sign," said Daniel. "There's a tunnel coming up."

"No, Daniel. Not *a tunnel* . . . ***The Tunnel!***"

As the Mercedes entered the tunnel, Prescott pulled to within a few feet of the Citroen. Armstrong had his gun trained on Churchill's head—Churchill saw this and turned away to fire on the Mercedes.

On the narrow two-lane road, separated by massive concrete pillars, the Citroen was violently rammed from behind, causing it to career into one of the pillars which spun it around before it was broadsided by Prescott's vehicle.

Dazed and unable to see well because of the blood running from his scalp into his eyes, Armstrong struggled to get out of the car. Just as he did so, he saw Dixon approach the vehicle and fire two shots into Prescott's chest. Scrambling for cover, Armstrong tripped over a tangled piece of bumper and fell to the ground. Before he could get to his feet, Dixon was hovering above him, his gun aimed at the policeman's head.

Fifty yards ahead, the Mercedes came to a stop, just in time for Olivia to see what was happening.

"Farewell, Inspector," Dixon said with a bloody smile.

Three quick shots rang out in the tunnel.

"Go, go, go!" screamed Olivia.

The Mercedes took off, and Daniel didn't look back.

Lying motionless on the roadway, Armstrong was stunned to see a hand pull Dixon's lifeless body from atop his own.

"Are you alright?" asked RMP Major Ripley.

"Yes, I think so," said Armstrong, struggling to his feet.

"Churchill?" he asked.

"Gone," said Ripley. "He stopped a car in the eastbound lane and took off."

"And the doctors?"

"Also gone . . . headed west," Ripley answered.

As his knees buckled, Armstrong was grabbed by Ripley to prevent him from falling.

The peal of approaching sirens became an eerie din as police and rescue vehicles entered the tunnel.

"Let's get you tended to, Chief Inspector," was the last thing Armstrong heard before losing consciousness.

Chapter Twenty-Two

Less than three hours after exiting the tunnel, Daniel and Olivia were standing at the host's table at Le Coup de Coeur, a private house of the 19th century, completely renovated in 2009 to serve as a unique boutique hotel in the heart of Brussels, Belgium.

"So, how'd I do?" asked Olivia, referring to the Google search she'd performed to find this place.

"Looks perfect," said Daniel. "Small, family operated, quiet . . ."

"And free Wi-Fi," Olivia cut in.

"You are without a doubt the most stunning computer geek I have ever met," said Daniel, before leaning over and kissing her.

"Ah, très romantique," said an elderly gentleman with wavy white hair beneath a costume closet beret. "You must be must be Monsieur et Madame Smith?" he said with a smile.

"Yep, that's us. The Smiths," said Daniel, giving Olivia a playful look. "We made a reservation on the Internet?"

"Oui. That is what Maxine told me. I am Maurice. May I help you to your room?"

"Don't we need to check in first?" asked Olivia.

"Why, are you going to steal the towels and go running out into the night?"

They all laughed together.

"Top of the stairs on your right," said Maurice, handing them a heavy metal key.

He spun on his heels and walked away. "Bon soir," he said as he went.

"Shall we?" asked Daniel, offering his arm.

"Let's," said Olivia, and the two of them strode up the stairs.

Upstairs in their two-room suite, Daniel unpacked, while Olivia flopped down on the bed.

"God, I'm exhausted," she said.

"I can understand that," said Daniel. "How often does your day consist of sightseeing, surgery in the street, a car chase through Paris with people shooting at you, fleeing to another country, and changing your name to Smith?"

"Was that all today? My god! We are one active couple."

Changing the subject, Daniel asked, "Olivia, did you see what happened in the tunnel?"

"Some of it," Olivia answered. "I heard the crash and turned around to see the two cars sliding and spinning around. I saw the man that Armstrong described as Dixon get out of his car and walk quickly toward Eddie's car and fire two shots. Then I saw him walk around to the other side of the car and aim his gun downward at something I could not see, and then I turned to you and said something about getting out of there."

"There were three more shots right then. Did you see that?" Daniel asked her.

"No," said Olivia. "That's all I saw or, at least, all I remember."

"Same here," said Daniel. "It was hard to see exactly what was going on with the wreckage blocking our view."

Olivia propped herself up on an elbow and asked the question they'd both been avoiding for hours.

"Do you think Dixon killed Eddie and his partner?"

Daniel thought for a moment.

"No." he said with conviction.

"And how did you come to that conclusion?" Olivia asked him.

"You saw Dixon fire the first two shots. I did not. I just heard them. Neither of us saw the last three shots being fired, but we both heard them."

"So?" said Olivia. "What are you getting at?"

"What did you hear, sweetheart?" he asked her.

You could almost smell Olivia's cerebral computer overheating. After a few moments, she got it.

"The first two shots and the next three shots didn't sound the same."

"And what does that tell you?" he asked.

"An acoustical variation because Dixon changed his position?"

"I don't think so," said Daniel. "It sounded to me like it was a different caliber weapon. Those last three shots weren't fired by Dixon."

"Who, then?" asked Olivia

"There are four possibilities," Daniel answered.

"Four? I count three. Churchill, Eddie and Eddie's partner. Who's the fourth?" she asked him.

"Work it," said Daniel.

"God, I am so dense. Must be because I'm tired. The fourth possible shooter was *someone else*, which is to say any one of the dozens of people whose cars were stopped by the accident, who, for whatever reason, happened to have a gun. It could have been a policeman, a gun collector, a serial killer, a road rage maniac—anyone."

"Anyone except Dixon," Daniel added. "Which gives me hope that our friends may still be alive."

At l'Hôpital Saint Vincent de Paul in central Paris, Chief Inspector Edward Armstrong of the Metropolitan Police Service, UK, was being questioned by local police about a car crash and two shootings that had occurred earlier that day in a Paris tunnel. Armstrong was not in the habit of lying to police investigators, yet there was only so much he could reveal with regard to this sticky situation.

Major Ripley, at Armstrong's suggestion, had bid a hasty retreat in advance of police and emergency vehicles arriving at the scene. It was too important that he be at liberty to protect Daniel and Olivia, should Churchill choose to continue his pursuit.

Though it had been more than four hours since the incident, Armstrong was being held for observation because he had suffered a concussion in the crash. The twelve stitches he had received to close the wound to his scalp were no big deal—nothing at all compared to the emergency surgery that Prescott was undergoing to try and save his life. The doctors were saying it could go either way.

In a small infirmary on the Left Bank, Phillip Churchill received treatment for a number of lacerations and contusions, including a blackened and swollen right eye, and was released. Though a description of Churchill had been given to the police by the young woman whose car he hijacked to make his escape, a man with a black eye in a city the size of Paris was not much to go on. He was presently holed up at a small hotel near the St-Germain Market.

Having spent much of the last hour trying, unsuccessfully, to contact Rousseau, who was inexplicably "unavailable," Churchill was rocked by the day's events and seeking comfort in a bottle of Cognac. The "cure" would prove to be effective for the next twelve hours.

Back in London, another Mr. Smith, more widely known as "Smitty," was doing his level best to locate Daniel and Olivia. He had already traced them to the Ritz Hotel in Paris, where Daniel used his Barclaycard credit card to check in, and he had spoken to members of the staff, who lead him to the concierge, who told him about the rental car. Now he was just waiting to hear back from Auto Europe, the company that rented the Mercedes. If they would provide the information he needed about the onboard GPS, he could find that car in a matter of minutes.

***

"Would you like to get some dinner?" Daniel asked Olivia, who was half asleep on the bed.

"I'm too tired," she answered.

"I can go out and get something and bring it back."

"If you walk out that door, I'm going to be asleep in two minutes, and if you wake me up when you return, I will make you pay for it," she answered.

"Ah, feisty. I like that about you."

"Daniel, I don't have an ounce of *feist* left in me. Please, just let me sleep."

Daniel removed Olivia's shoes, covered her with a comforter, and kissed her forehead.

"Mmm," was her response.

Daniel went downstairs to find an attractive, fiftyish, redheaded woman, sitting on a plush, velvet loveseat, a book in one hand, and a glass of Merlot in the other.

"Ah, you must be Monsieur Smith," she said with a smile.

"Daniel," he answered with an embarrassed grin.

"Bienvenue. I am Maxine. Can I offer you a glass of wine?"

"That would be wonderful," Daniel answered.

As Maxine went to the nearby wine bar, Daniel moved to an armchair across from the loveseat.

"Compliments of the house," she told him as she handed him a glass of the aromatic red wine.

"Merci beaucoup," Daniel answered.

"So, Daniel, what brings you to Brussels; or should I say, what is it you are trying to get away from?"

Daniel was caught off guard by the question. "I beg your pardon?" he said.

"It has been my observation that people don't come to places as much as they go away from other places. It is a question of perspective. Did you come to Brussels because this is where you most want to be, or did you leave somewhere else because it was the last place you wanted to be? In short, are you a man who doesn't know if he's coming or going?"

Daniel smiled, took a sip of wine, and considered the odd but interesting question.

"I am definitely going," he decided.

"And your wife, if she is your wife—going with you or just coming along?"

"Going with me," he said without hesitation. "And if I may anticipate your next question which you already know the answer to, where we are going is *away*."

"Very good, Daniel. You have a quick mind."

Maxine went back to the wine bar, fixed a board of baguette, cheese and olives, grabbed the bottle of Merlot, and returned to her seat.

"So you do not starve," she said to him.

"Merci," he answered and went straight for the bread and cheese.

"So, Daniel Smith, who are you?" she asked with a coy smile.

Daniel chewed and swallowed some bread and cheese, refilled his wine glass, and spoke frankly to this stranger who was his best friend in Belgium.

"I am Dr. Daniel Whittemore, a doctor on staff at the Oxford Radcliffe Hospital outside of London. Mrs. Smith, who is not my wife, but very definitely the love of my life, is Doctor Olivia Franklin, an oncologist specializing in childhood leukemia, and also a princess whom I have rescued from imprisonment by usurpers in the castle tower, so as to practice my chivalry and my commitment to the true Royal Family."

It was becoming apparent to both Maxine and Daniel that the wine was working its magic in a delightful and much needed way.

"Bravo, Sir Daniel," Maxine said while clapping approvingly. "A fitting fairytale to be played out in part at Le Coup de Coeur. How may I serve you, my liege?"

"Do you have any more of this fine Merlot?" Daniel asked.

While Maxine uncorked another bottle, Daniel took a moment to consider the situation. Clearly, Maxine was uninvolved in his uniquely bizarre situation, so why not open up to her a little bit. It might just clarify his own thinking or, at the very least, provide some respite from the incredible adventure that he and Olivia found themselves consumed by.

"Daniel," she said with a very serious look on her face. "Lean over and let me look into your eyes."

Daniel did as instructed, enjoying what seemed to be a highly metaphysical and altogether entertaining experience of growing inebriation.

"You are a wholesome man—one to be trusted," she concluded. "As such, you can trust me completely. Tell me of the peril that the princess is in."

The Right Honorable Christopher Geidt was preparing for his morning meeting with the Queen when the Assistant Private Secretary, Mr. Douglas King, entered his office.

"Sir, I think you should have a look at this," said King, handing his boss a card that had arrived that morning addressed to the Queen.

The Private Secretary, an official position since the late 1800s, read Armstrong's message and looked up at King.

"What do we know of this?" he asked.

"Churchill and Dixon are reported to be whereabouts unknown, and Armstrong is in fact a chief inspector with Scotland Yard, currently on a case in France," said the Assistant Private Secretary.

"And what does the RMP say about this?" Geidt asked him.

"Well, that's the strange thing," said King. "I spoke with an RMP Major by the name of Blackstone, and he said he could only discuss this with you directly. I took the liberty of scheduling an appointment with him at 10:00 a.m."

Geidt looked at his watch, which read 9:40 a.m., then glanced at the agenda he had set for his meeting with the Queen at 11:00 a.m.

"Very well," said Geidt. "Tell the Deputy Private Secretary that I'd like to see him immediately."

"As you wish, sir," said King before exiting the room.

Geidt glanced again at the message then picked up the phone.

"Get me Sir Paul Stephenson," he said, referring to the Commissioner of the Metropolitan Police Service.

Chapter Twenty-Three

Armstrong had just finished telling Rousseau about the death of his friend, Hugh Dixon, and the near-fatal shooting of Inspector Nigel Prescott.

"I am at a loss for words," said Rousseau. "There can be no doubt that I contributed to these events, and, quite frankly, I am in shock. Why would Dixon lie to me and use me in this way?"

"He was convinced by Churchill and, I believe, a member of the British Royal Family that the Franklin woman is a threat to the crown—a threat so great that she has to be eliminated," said Armstrong.

"Then it must be true," said Rousseau. "Hugh was not a man to do such a thing unless there was a most compelling reason."

"The reason is quite compelling," Armstrong admitted. "But the underlying facts are in error. Olivia Franklin is a threat to no one. To the contrary, she is the innocent victim of a nefarious plot that started decades ago—a series of royal mistakes that have come back to haunt the House of Windsor and betray their arrogance."

"And you can tell me nothing more about the nature of this plot and how a good man like Hugh Dixon could be driven to the point of shooting your friend, Prescott, and attempting to kill you, Franklin, and her companion?"

Armstrong paused for a moment to gather his thoughts.

"I am a policeman through and through," he began. "I am sworn to uphold the law and protect the innocent, no matter how uncomfortable or embarrassing that might be to others. Kings and queens and presidents and prime ministers are not above the law. Not ever, under any circumstances, no matter how easy it might seem to justify their actions. I believe, having studied your file, that you are such a man as well —a dedicated policeman who is guided in all things by the law. Churchill and Dixon have no such allegiance. They are loyal not to laws but to the monarchy, and they do not question orders from the Royal Family, no matter how ill-conceived they may be. I hope you can understand that, because it is the only explanation I can offer."

Rousseau rose from his chair and paced around his office.

"So, what now?" he finally asked.

"We do what men like you and I always do. We see that the guilty are brought to justice under the law."

There was a long silence before Rousseau spoke again.

"Tell me, mon ami, what can I do to help you make this right?" he asked.

Olivia awakened at 3:00 a.m., while Daniel had been asleep for barely an hour. In the sitting room of their suite, she sat at her laptop, doing search after search on the Internet, sometimes switching from Google to Yahoo to Bing to check for variations in the results. She had searched the Royal Family, Phillip Churchill, Edward Armstrong, Brussels, Belgium, Princess Diana, GPS, her father and mother, in vitro fertilization, Prince Charles, the European Union Customs and Immigration, Kate Middleton, and local news for Paris, London, and Oxford.

At 5:00 a.m., she narrowed the field to a single subject: her brother, Prince William.

There are a thousand different ways to search for anything on the Internet—actually, there are an infinite number of ways. *Prince William Bio* will yield different results than *Prince William History, Prince William Background, Prince William Friends, Prince William Doctors,* or even just plain old *Prince William.* The fact is that the search terms *Prince William*

Pajamas, Prince William Buddies, Prince William Potato Chips, and *Prince William from Mars* will all bring up results, and any one of them might give you the factoid that will send you in the direction you want to go. Unfortunately, as truly amazing as search engines have become, they all rely on the human brain to provide the all important filters that separate *chicken recipes* from the urban myth—*Kentucky Fried Chicken changed its name to KFC because they stopped using real chicken in favor of artificial chicken grown in test tubes in their secret laboratory.* Over ten million Google searches have been done on that very subject, and an astounding number of people have concluded that it's true.

Though Olivia and Daniel had both done macro, generic searches of Prince William when they were in Paris, Olivia decided that it might be more fruitful to take a more microscopic look at William's life by going year by year through his personal history.

Beginning on June 21, 1982 with his birth at Saint Mary's Hospital in Paddington, Olivia read every news story pertaining to her brother as they unfolded in a given year.

In his first year of life, little was reported of a factual nature, other than his christening by the Archbishop of Canterbury in August.

In 1983, he became a jet-setter, traveling with his parents to New Zealand and Canada, though few other details of his life were made public.

In '84, he went back to Saint Mary's to meet his newborn brother Harry in September. He also appeared in a lengthy video, posing for the first time for photojournalists, who revealed to the world a precocious two year-old, kicking a football and enjoying the swing set in the garden of his home.

And so it went, year by year—William and Harry banging on a piano in a home video in 1985—William serving as a page boy at his Uncle Andrew's wedding in '86—more pictures in the British press of the young princes in '87—a spread in People magazine in 1988, depicting the perfect family—and so on.

Interestingly, from 1990 until the last year or so, fewer and fewer pictures and stories appeared in the press as the family sought to insulate William from public scrutiny. It's one thing to be an adorable toddler for all the world to see, and quite another for an eight, nine, or ten-year-old to be in the limelight.

"Buggers," said Olivia, as she could find almost nothing about William during the five years he spent at the Ludgrove School in Berkshire, and even less during his time at Eton College. Though there was news footage of William on his first day of college, there was little else, save for a few pictures of him playing water polo and soccer.

Particularly frustrating to Olivia were comments by a BBC reporter on William's first day at Eton—a mention of the Prince not being lonely because several of his classmates at Ludgrove were attending Eton as well. No names were mentioned.

These friends from early childhood through college were exactly what Olivia was looking for, but no targeted search such as *Prince William's Friends, Classmates, Teammates,* or any such thing revealed even the tiniest lead. Such was also the case for William's time at St. Andrews University, where the only classmate mentioned in the press was his on-again, off-again girlfriend, Kate Middleton.

Around 7:00 a.m, Olivia began reading everything she could find about her brother's training at the Royal Military Academy at Sandhurst, right up to his graduation in December 1996. While most of the world remembers where they were and what they were doing on August 31st of the following year, when news reports of Diana's death swept through global media, few people are aware that William's world was shattered yet again when his friend, mentor, and de facto guardian at Sandhurst died in a fiery car crash some time later.

"That's it," said Olivia, staring at the computer screen before her. She could hardly believe it, but she had found her intermediary.

"Bonjour," said Churchill into the telephone. "Monsieur Rousseau, s'il vous plait . . . Phillip Churchill, calling."

"Un moment," said the secretary.

Churchill was put on hold where he listened to several seconds of Charles Aznavour singing La Boheme, followed by a series of clicks, then nothing.

"FUCK!" said Churchill, realizing that the call was being traced. He slammed down the phone and proceeded to pack up his few belongings.

Secretary Geidt and Major Blackstone were wrapping up their meeting, and neither man was all that happy about the current situation.

"I'm afraid that's all we know," said Blackstone apologetically.

"Well, it is wholly insufficient," said the Secretary. "Two of the Queen's most trusted and loyal servants are running around killing people, and you can't tell me why?"

"I can't tell you why, because I don't know why," said the Major. "Perhaps Commissioner Stephenson can shed more light on the subject. It seems that his man, Armstrong, is the only one who knows all the details."

"Well, Stephenson will be here shortly," said Geidt, rising from his chair. "Right now, I have to brief the Queen, and I can assure you that her Majesty will be most unhappy with what I'm about to tell her. Good day to you, Major."

"Not enough time," said Rousseau's tech, Marquand. "I think he may have tumbled to the trace and hung up. If that's the case, I doubt we'll be hearing from him again."

Rousseau looked at Armstrong, his eyes curled into question marks.

"We can't afford to let him isolate," said Armstrong. "I believe the man is very close to insane at this point, and we should not underestimate the lengths to which he will go. I feel quite certain that if he had reason to believe Olivia Franklin was on a plane to anywhere, he would have no qualms about taking down the flight into a heavily populated area."

Rousseau rubbed his chin for several seconds, trying to discern a move in this deadly game of chess.

"Monsieur Marquand," he finally said. "Are you happy working here?"

"Yes, Sir . . . of course, Sir," Marquand answered nervously. "Why do you ask?"

"Because you look to me like an under-paid, disgruntled employee who sees an opportunity to enrich himself in the free market."

Marquand was momentarily in shock.

"I like it," said Armstrong, understanding where Rousseau was going. "Let me speak to my tech wizard in London. I think he and Monsieur Marquand will make a lovely couple."

"Your Majesty," said the Royal Attendant. "The Private Secretary is in the anteroom."

"Show him in," said the Queen of England.

Chapter Twenty-Four

"Daniel, wake up," Olivia said loudly, hurling herself onto the bed. "Wake up!"

"What? What is it?" he responded, jolted awake, and startled by her tone. "What's wrong?"

"Nothing," she answered. "I think I found her."

"Who her?" said Daniel, half asleep. He propped himself up, trying to shake off the cobwebs.

"The intermediary . . . I think I found her," said Olivia. "Her name is Susie Roberts."

"And who, pray tell, is Susie Roberts?"

"Susie Roberts is the widow of Major Lex Roberts, whose military vehicle was blown to bits by an improvised explosive device outside of Kandahar, Afghanistan in 2007."

Daniel just stared at her for a moment, and then said, "Good morning, love."

"Yes. Good morning. Now, listen," said Olivia. "Lex Roberts was an up and coming star in the British Army. He was specially selected to be William's platoon commander at Sandhurst. The two of them became very close at the academy. Major Roberts was his friend, his mentor, and something of a father figure to William. Are you listening?"

"I am," said Daniel. "As best as I can with this hangover. I'm afraid I had a bit too much wine last night."

"That's nice, honey," said Olivia. "Now get this . . . when Major Roberts was killed, Prince William was devastated, according to a wide variety of sources. The first thing he did was reach out to Major Roberts' widow . . ."

"Susie," said Daniel.

"That's correct," said Olivia, continuing with the story. "William and Susie have remained close since the Major died. She and her two girls lead a fairly normal life in Kent. She is not upper crust, not a celebrity, not particularly well known, and a friend of the Prince."

"So, you think that this Susie Roberts is A: approachable, and B: has access to the Prince?"

"I do," said Olivia. "She is exactly the kind of person I've been looking for—someone I can probably get to with little difficulty—someone who has the Prince's ear."

"And what makes you think, what with William and Kate's wedding coming up in just a few weeks, that she has access to William at the moment?" he asked.

"Because the wedding guest list has just been released, and Susie Roberts is on it."

"Do you mind if I take a shower and we talk about this over coffee?" said Daniel, climbing out of bed.

"Cute butt," Olivia answered.

Olivia walked over to the window and her eyes filled up. She realized just how much she missed her parents. She said softly, "They only knew how hurt I was when Daniel and I broke up. Mom and Dad, I love you. I wish you could see how happy I am."

In London, Smitty had just received the information he was waiting for about the onboard GPS in the Mercedes. He spent a couple of minutes tapping on the keyboard of his computer, then picked up the phone and called Armstrong.

"The Mercedes is parked in front of 20 Rue Bixio in Paris," said Smitty.

"And why is that?" asked Armstrong.

Because that was the closest place to ditch the car with its shattered rear window and multiple bullet holes and pick up another rental," Smitty explained.

"And that rental is?" asked Armstrong.

"A silver BMW X1, rented from the Avis office two blocks down at 5 Rue Bixio, currently parked at the Place de la Vieille Halle aux Bles in Brussels."

"Good work, Smitty. Keep an eye on it, and be sure to keep Marquand informed."

"Do you think that's a good idea, sir?" Smitty asked.

"At the moment, it's our only idea," Armstrong answered before ending the call.

Major Ripley was making his way to a small city in southern France—a popular winter sport destination at the base of the French Alps. He was relying on Armstrong's hunch that Daniel and Olivia would show up there, and he intended to be in place before they arrived.

"If they arrive," he said to himself.

He was still in a state of disbelief over the whole affair—Churchill killing at least four people, including his friend, Ryan Wright—Dixon, the RMP legend, whom he himself had shot—the ongoing pursuit of Doctors Franklin and Whittemore, two innocent people who had done nothing at all to provoke this insanity.

"But, who among us is innocent?" he asked philosophically.

"Drive, Ripley. Just drive," he finally said before switching the car's radio.

Daniel and Olivia were downstairs having breakfast. If nothing else, Le Coup de Coeur was known for its lavish breakfast, prepared and served by the innkeeper, Maurice, who insisted that his guests begin each day with an assortment of meats, soufflés, fruits, and freshly baked breads and pastries.

"Everything is satisfactory?" asked the white-haired old gent.

"Fabulous," said Olivia through a mouthful of sausage.

"Excellent," said Maurice. "I have a fresh pot of coffee brewing. I will be right back."

"So, where were we?" said Olivia, buttering a croissant.

"You were saying that you were surprised that we haven't heard from Armstrong," Daniel answered.

"Well, I assume that if he were able to contact us, he would. Don't you agree?"

"I'm not so sure," said Daniel. "Given that with all our precautions, Churchill and Dixon still found and nearly killed us in Paris, he might have decided that it's just too risky to call or email."

"I suppose," said Olivia, pondering the situation. "But where does that leave us, Daniel? If Churchill and or Dixon are still alive, you know they'll come after us. Your friend Armstrong must know that, too. So why would he leave us out in the cold?"

"I don't believe he would," Daniel answered. "Eddie wouldn't do that. We're missing something."

They both sat silently for nearly a minute.

"Olivia!" said Daniel.

"Daniel!" said Olivia.

"I need you to do something."

"Anything, my prince," she answered with a seductive smile.

"I need you to access those remarkable memory banks in that exquisite brain of yours and try to recall, word for word, the phone conversation you had with Armstrong during the chase in Paris."

"Hmm," said Olivia, booting up that part of her brain. "As I recall, when I heard the phone ring I was startled, then frightened, then past

164

frightened and beginning to be relaxed, and by the time I answered the call, I had moved on to whimsy. I said something like, 'Bonjour, Paris Tours.'"

"I believe that's exactly what you said," Daniel responded. "Good. Keep going."

"Well . . ." she began. "He said hello . . . then, he asked to speak to you . . . then, I told him you were busy trying to get away from the people that were bent on killing us and glibly asked him if I could take a message . . ."

"Yes," said Daniel.

"And then, he said that he and his partner were just minutes away . . . that they were coming to help us . . . that Churchill and Dixon were determined to kill us—something I had already concluded—and then . . . that he had a message for you."

"What message?" Daniel asked. "Try to be precise."

Olivia exhaled loudly and squinted her eyes just a bit.

"He said something strange . . . something about the Olympics."

"Reach for it, sweetheart. It's in there."

"He said to tell Daniel that his favorite sporting event is the Winter Olympics . . . and that it made France what it is today."

Daniel looked puzzled—not the response Olivia was hoping for.

"Are you sure that's what he said?" Daniel asked.

"As sure as I am that I'm going to finish that mushroom soufflé you haven't touched."

"Hmm," said Daniel, drawing a blank.

Churchill had picked up another rental and was waiting for instructions from the palace. Without Dixon and Rousseau, his chances of finding Olivia were rather bleak, and he was hoping for some additional support from His Royal Highness. In the end, his only hope of survival rested on killing the pretender and every trace of this royal mess. If he could accomplish that, he was certain the family would provide for him, and he could go off somewhere and live out his life in peace. Serving the family was everything, and it had always been understood that those who faithfully served would be rewarded.

He was just passing the Louvre when his phone signaled that he had a text message. He pulled over by the hideous, glass pyramid, I. M. Pei's monstrosity and read the text.

Place de la Vieille Halle aux Bles in Brussels.

🐾

"We need to draw Churchill to a place of our choosing and neutralize him there," said Armstrong to Rousseau. "Brussels is as good a place as any."

"I agree," said Rousseau. "I will make arrangements."

🐾

As Olivia and Daniel were about finished with breakfast, Maxine appeared with a glorious smile on her face.

"Oh, my," she said, staring at Olivia. "Daniel, Daniel, Daniel. You are, indeed, a prince among men."

"Uh, Olivia . . . I'd like you to meet Maxine. She's . . ."

"She is honored to be in your presence," Maxine said with a deep curtsey.

"Daniel?" said Olivia.

"It's okay, Liv. Maxine is . . ."

"Your devoted servant," Maxine cut in. Then, turning to Daniel . . . "If I didn't see it with my own eyes, I wouldn't believe it, Sir Daniel."

Maxine quickly pulled a chair from another table and sat down with Daniel and Olivia.

"Anybody ever tell you that you look exactly like the late Princess of Wales?" she said to Olivia.

"Daniel!"

"Oh, it's alright, love," said Maxine pulling a flask from her purse. "We are all Musketeers."

"It's okay, Olivia," said Daniel, putting a reassuring hand on her arm. "Maxine is going to help us. She is quite knowledgeable and trustworthy beyond reproach. Can I have a swig of that, Max?"

Olivia put her head in her hands, closed her eyes, and did something that is somewhere near the middle of laughing and crying.

"Alright, Madame Trustworthy and Knowledgeable," Olivia said. "What does the phrase Winter Olympics mean to you?"

"This is a real question?" asked Maxine.

"As real as a bullet in the head," Olivia said.

Maxine took a pull from her flask and smiled.

"Jean-Claude Killy . . . the greatest skier ever . . .1968 . . . Grenoble, France."

Daniel and Olivia just stared at each other.

"Can I have a bit of that?" Olivia asked Maxine as she grabbed the flask from her hand.

Chapter Twenty-Five

In a helicopter headed north from Paris to Brussels, Armstrong and Rousseau were going over the operation that was little more than an hour away. The objectives were twofold: First, and foremost, was to secure Olivia and Daniel. Second, and just as important, was to take down Churchill.

"The two go hand-in-hand," said Armstrong. "Daniel and Olivia will never be safe until Churchill is neutralized, and the sooner we do that, the greater the likelihood that we will be able to contain the mess he has created."

"I agree in part," said Rousseau. "Daniel and Olivia must be safe; Churchill must be stopped, and I am not at all sure that the trail of wreckage that stretches from a Paris tunnel to London and Oxford can still be contained. People are dead, and questions are being asked, both in France and in England."

"I understand," said Armstrong. "But all we can do is all we can do, and today, we must do our best to meet our objectives."

Rousseau pulled out his gun, checked the magazine and chamber, and holstered his weapon.

In the Private Secretary's office in Buckingham Palace, Sir Paul Stephenson, Commissioner of the Metropolitan Police Service, was meeting the Queen's principal liaison for all who serve her.

"So, you're telling me that you don't know what this is all about, and you expect me to believe that, Commissioner?" said Secretary Geidt.

"Mr. Secretary, I have told you all that I know. What you believe is something I have no control over," said Sir Paul. "Chief Inspector Armstrong has my complete confidence, and when he tells me that this matter is so sensitive and threatening to the Crown that he dare not even tell me the details, I fully accept that. All I can tell you is that Lt. Colonel Churchill has been implicated in four murders—Arthur and Elizabeth Franklin, RMP Major Ryan Wright, whom I believe you knew, and MPS Constable Bruce Jackson, whom I've known since he was a cadet. Beyond that, we know that Hugh Dixon, former RMP Commander, was shot and killed in Paris while attempting the murder of Chief Inspector Armstrong and Inspector Prescott, and that Phillip Churchill is still on the loose and, presumably, a continuing threat to Doctors Franklin and Whittemore."

"And this note to the Queen?" said Secretary Geidt, sliding Armstrong's message across his desk. "How is Her Majesty supposed to put an end to this if you don't know what's going on."

"It is Armstrong's belief that Churchill and Dixon were acting under orders," said the Commissioner.

"Orders from whom?" asked the Private Secretary.

"Come now, Mr. Geidt. We both know that any such orders could only have come from the Royal Family," Sir Paul pointed out.

"Well, the Queen knows nothing about this, and I'm sure she will be just thrilled to learn that the Commissioner of the Metropolitan Police Service doesn't seem to know much more."

"Funny," said Sir Paul. "That's pretty much what Armstrong said to me."

"I'm all set," said Olivia, zipping up her duffel.

"One minute," said Daniel, placing their laptops into the special carry-on bags they had purchased in London. "Okay, let's go, he said, grabbing all their bags and heading for the door.

Downstairs, they were met by Maxine and Maurice, who had a basket of food and wine for Daniel and Olivia.

"Monsieur," said Maxine to Daniel. "If I wasn't so crazy about this sexy, old man here, I would kiss you hard on the lips, right in front of your Princess."

She kissed him, first on one cheek, then the other, then again on the first.

"Thank you, Maxine. You are truly a gem, and we are forever in your debt," said Daniel.

Maxine turned to Olivia and just stared at her for a second before grabbing her hand and leading her away for a private conversation.

"She is, how you say, the most exciting woman I have ever known," said Maurice. "Ah, Maxine . . . she makes my blood boil."

"You know that she loves you very much," said Daniel.

"No, no, no, Monsieur. If she really loved me, would she keep me up all night?" Maurice said with a sly grin.

Daniel smiled in understanding and then looked at his watch.

"Dr. Franklin, we have to go," he shouted.

"Coming, my prince," Olivia answered.

The helicopter carrying Armstrong and Rousseau had just landed at Ecole Fondamentale de l'Heliport, in the heart of Brussels, when Marquand called.

"The car is on the move," said Marquand to Rousseau. "They are headed south toward the motorway back to Paris."

"Stay with it, Jacques," said Rousseau.

"We must hurry," he said to Armstrong as they climbed into an awaiting car with a driver.

Rousseau barked some orders in French, and the driver took off at high speed. A minute later, he steered the car over the steel spikes at the heliport's parking lot entrance, blowing all four tires.

Armstrong looked at Rousseau with an expression that spoke volumes.

***

Car on the move, said the text message on Churchill's phone.

"Blimey," he shouted to no one.

He was less than two minutes from where the car had been parked for more than twenty-four hours—now this.

Strong signal. Take Ave du Port South. Silver BMW X1 French tags 121JL.

***

Daniel and Olivia were headed south toward France. They had programmed the GPS to bypass Paris and plot a route to Grenoble that was unlikely to attract attention. It was a good plan, unless someone had access to their GPS.

***

Armstrong was on the phone to Smitty in London, explaining the situation.

Rousseau had already spoken to Marquand and was currently talking to an operative in Luxembourg.

Not paying attention to his surroundings, Armstrong was almost run down by an Audi carrying a businessman who very nearly had a heart attack at the near miss. Armstrong dropped his phone, picked it up, saw the silver RX6 insignia on the side of the car, and pulled his gun.

172

"Out!" he shouted to the driver and his passenger.

"Come on," he said to Rousseau.

"What are we doing?" Rousseau asked as he jumped into the passenger side of the car while Armstrong took the wheel and the former passengers ran for their lives.

"What we are doing," Armstrong said calmly, "is confiscating one of the fastest production cars in the world."

"Could you speed it up?" said Rousseau with a smile.

The text message on Churchill's phone read: *E411 South–Two Miles ahead.*

Churchill stomped on the accelerator and passed four cars ahead of him.

"We end it now," he said to no one.

"Are you sure?" asked Olivia as Daniel turned onto the E411 motorway towards Luxembourg.

"Pretty sure," Daniel answered. "This Olympics bit is just the sort of thing that Eddie would do. It's like when we were in school. He'd pass me a note in class that said 'Mary, Mary, quite . . .' and I knew to meet him in the garden behind Mary Michael's house after school."

"Mary Michaels? Who's Mary Michaels?" Olivia asked with a sneer.

"Mary Michaels was the over-developed twelve year-old who would go home after school and change her clothes without drawing the curtains."

"Daniel Whittemore, I always suspected that before you were a dirty old man, you were a dirty young boy," Olivia commented.

"Excuse me! I happen to be a dirty *young* man," Daniel responded. "Before that, I was just a boy," he added.

Olivia was silent for a moment, just smiling and looking out the passenger side window.

"Daniel?" she said, gazing into the side-view mirror. "Is that red Renault following us?"

"They are on the motorway toward Luxembourg," said Marquand to Rousseau.

"Un moment," said Rousseau. He programmed the GPS in the Audi to plot a route to Luxembourg from their current location.

"E411 South?" he asked Marquand.

"Oui," said Marquand. "About five miles ahead of you."

"Any sign of Churchill?" Rousseau asked him.

"None," Marquand answered. "I have not been able to make contact with him or pick up his trail."

"Call back in five minutes," Rousseau instructed. "We are going to make a run at them."

Rousseau looked at Armstrong, who fastened his seat belt and floored it.

Daniel moved into the right hand lane and slowed to see what the Renault would do. In a matter of seconds, it passed them on the left and kept on going. Remaining in the slow lane, Daniel watched as one car after another passed them by.

"It looks like we are okay," he said to Olivia as he made his way to the far left lane and picked up speed.

"Sorry," said Olivia. "I guess I'm a little paranoid at this point."

174

"It's not paranoia when people are actually trying to kill you," he pointed out.

✹

About 100 meters ahead, Churchill saw the silver BMW change lanes. Three seconds later, he got a text confirming what he already knew.

"Be patient," he said to himself. "Stay back. Keep your distance. Don't let them know you are here. Stalk them. Hunt them. Wait for the right moment before making the kill. A sure kill. It must be a sure kill." His eyes were crazy.

Churchill's excruciating headache was more than enough of a reminder of the events in the Paris tunnel. Now, he was on a high-speed motorway and alone in the car. He would wait until the perfect opportunity presented itself.

"The perfect opportunity," he said to himself. "It must be perfect. Perfect."

✹

Armstrong was driving well over the speed limit when he spotted the silver BMW. He immediately slowed to confer with Rousseau.

Just then the BMW's right turn signal went on and it appeared to be slowing as it approached an upcoming exit ramp. Armstrong and Rousseau exchanged puzzled looks. The moment was quickly shattered when a car in front of them made a wild maneuver to get behind the BMW as it exited the highway. Armstrong slowed again and then followed the two cars around the bend of the exit ramp.

Still keeping his distance, he soon determined that the car in front of his was definitely following Daniel and Olivia's car.

"Slow down and put on your left turn signal," said Rousseau. They both watched as the two cars ahead increased their distance and

175

disappeared around a bend to the right. Armstrong quickly sped up and made the same turn, only to see the two vehicles parked in front of a restaurant. Not a second later, the doors to the BMW opened and a white-haired old man and an attractive redhead climbed out.

"Incroyable!" said Rousseau, realizing that someone else had been driving the BMW.

Armstrong jumped from the Audi, pulled his gun and ran towards the other vehicle just as Churchill was stepping out. The Chief Inspector fired one shot, which missed Churchill as he dove back into his car and sped off in a cloud of smoking tires. Armstrong lowered his weapon and walked slowly toward the man and woman.

"Inspector Armstrong, I presume," said Maxine.

Armstrong was dumbfounded.

"I have a message for you from the Princess," she continued, leaving Armstrong speechless.

"She said to pack warm clothes. It is still winter in the Alps."

Chapter Twenty-Six

The city of Grenoble is not a particularly bustling place, especially at the end of March, as winter turns to spring. In 1968, the weather did its best in southern France to accommodate the Winter Olympic Games X. It was a brilliant event for all of the citizens of France, as native son Jean-Claude Killy dazzled the world by dominating the games, owning all three downhill events and walking away with three gold medals. Many have said it was the greatest day for France since the liberation of Paris on August 19, 1944.

When Daniel and Olivia rolled into Grenoble, a little after 10:00 that night, it took RMP major Richard Ripley about two seconds to spot them.

"Inspector Armstrong has been expecting you," said Ripley as he leaned into Daniel's window at the entrance of the Hotel Angleterre. "Please follow me."

Ripley helped them from the car, gathered their bags, tipped the valet 20 euro, and hailed a taxi.

"Hotel Europole," he said as they climbed into the taxi.

"Chief Inspector Armstrong will meet us here before midnight. Have you eaten?"

"Actually, I've been holding out for fondue," said Olivia. "Do they have that here?"

Ripley just smiled as the taxi climbed the hill toward their hotel.

"I'm telling you, that was Churchill," said Armstrong as he swerved between vehicles on his run to Grenoble.

"I don't understand," said Rousseau. "My man, Marquand, said he has had no contact with Churchill. How did he find that car?"

Armstrong pulled out his phone and hit 1 on his speed dial.

"It's Armstrong," he said officiously. "Yes, Commissioner . . . I'm sure they are quite confused at the moment . . . no sir, I'm afraid he got away . . . yes, I imagine the Private Secretary is quite displeased, and I know what that means . . . no . . . no . . . no, Sir, but I believe he had help, and I'm afraid it's one of ours . . . yes, Sir, thank you, Sir Paul."

"Well?" said Rousseau.

"Call your man, Marquand," said Armstrong. "Unless I'm mistaken, we won't be hearing from Smitty again."

In the Queen's office in Buckingham Palace, Her Majesty Elizabeth II asked the Private Secretary to excuse himself.

She sat in complete silence for several minutes before summoning her lady in waiting.

"Yes, Your Majesty," said the young woman who sat just outside the doorway to the room.

"Mrs. Welch, would you bring me my personal phone book?"

Carole Welch, the Queen's lady in waiting, was aghast.

"Your Majesty, if you need to make a call . . ."

"Mrs. Welch, my phone book, please."

Following their dinner of romaine and radish salad, a mix and match of cheese and beef fondue, and a parade of cocktails that lasted through the dessert tray, which wasn't touched, Ripley led Daniel and Olivia from the Brasserie du Palais to their suite in the Hotel Europole.

Olivia was tired from the long car ride but at the same time driven to get on the Internet and gather more information about her brother and his bride-to-be, as well as Susie Roberts, the woman she was hoping to enlist as a conduit to Prince William.

"Do you want to go to bed?" Daniel asked from his position on the couch.

"In a little while," Olivia answered.

She wasn't sure what she was looking for. She just knew that if this was going to work she needed to know everything about the wedding plans, the parties, the parade route, Susie Roberts, wedding etiquette, and protocol. In the back of her mind, she was thinking all the while that she didn't want to "use" Susie Roberts, nor did she want to compromise her privacy in any way. Olivia felt that if she could simply sit down with the woman and establish a rapport, maybe she could gain her confidence and help.

After about an hour of surfing the web, Olivia was about to turn in for the night when she ran into an article from BBC News Online which set off such a cacophony of alarms, sirens, and bells in her head that she couldn't believe Daniel slept through it. The headline read:

Royal Succession Reform Being Discussed.

According to Deputy Prime Minister Nick Clegg, the government has been consulting Commonwealth countries about changing the laws on royal succession. At present, the law of primogeniture means male heirs accede to the throne before any older sisters.

Mr. Clegg, who is responsible for constitutional reform, told the BBC the issue would "require careful thought." But, he said both he and (Prime Minister) David Cameron were "sympathetic" to changing rules.

"My own personal view is that, in this day and age, the idea that only a man should ascend to the throne, I think, would strike most people as a little old-fashioned," said Clegg.

Olivia's "ah-ha moment" went well beyond a few seconds as she came to understand for the first time why people were so determined to kill her.

"Son of a bitch!" she said out loud.

Olivia got up from the table, walked to the door, pulled it open, and was startled to see Armstrong about to knock.

"Join me for a nightcap?" he asked her.

"Absolutely!" she answered.

"How are you holding up?" Armstrong asked Olivia as they settled into a booth in the hotel bar.

"Not sure," said Olivia. "If I stop to think about it, it gets rather overwhelming. Everything is so surreal. Is this really happening?"

"I'm afraid so," said Armstrong. "And I think I understand what you're saying. It is all quite bizarre, and I'm not dealing with half the issues you're confronting."

"Am I confronting them, Eddie? It feels to me like I'm just running," said Olivia.

Armstrong signaled the waitress, who quickly took their order.

"No, my dear," Armstrong continued. "What you are doing is bravely handling an awful lot of stuff that came out of nowhere and turned your whole world upside down. In my view, you are doing it extremely well. Your biological mother was one of the most beloved women in the world. Now, today she lives on in her only daughter, you Olivia. You not only look like Princess Diana but she is a part of you…flesh and blood. If Diana could come back to us in some way it would create bedlam. From my understanding, the laws of succession require you to have been born not out of wedlock, be a practicing Protestant and not be married to a Catholic. By my calculations, you would be the heir to the throne before William and Harry."

"I don't even want to think about that. If it were not for Daniel, I would never be able to handle any of this," Olivia answered. "I don't know if he mentioned it, but we are very much in love."

"I've known that since day one," Armstrong answered. "The question is, what is it going to take to make the two of you safe once and for all?"

"I gather Churchill is still on the loose," she said, more as a statement than a question. Armstrong just looked at her.

As Olivia sipped a very strong Irish coffee, the Chief Inspector tried to fill her in on all that had happened—Dixon's death, Prescott's near-fatal shooting, Churchill's escape and reemergence on the motorway near Luxembourg, and most importantly, the Queen's recent entrance into the picture.

"The Queen is involved?" Olivia said in total shock. "I need Daniel to wake up."

"To a degree," Armstrong explained. "She's been briefed on everything that's happened, but as far as I know, she isn't aware that it's all because of you and your royal lineage."

Olivia didn't say anything for a few moments.

"Did you see the news about the government looking into changing the laws governing succession?" Olivia asked.

"I did," said Armstrong. "It explains a lot."

"Let me make one thing clear," said Olivia. Then she paused, seeing Daniel walking into the bar.

Daniel gave his old friend, Eddie, a bear hug and sat down next to Olivia.

"I thought I might find you here," he said.

After the waitress took his drink order, Olivia continued.

"Can we do a quick head count?" she began. "Who knows the whole story about the circumstances of my birth?"

Armstrong took a pull of scotch and laid it out for them.

"When you think about it, the whole business is still remarkably well contained," Armstrong told them. "Given the number of RMPs involved, my people at Scotland Yard, Rousseau, Commissioner Stephenson, the Private Secretary and the Queen—outside of the three of us and Inspector Prescott, the only other people who know are Churchill and whoever he's working for."

"And do you have any theories about who that might be?" Daniel asked.

Armstrong paused, looked at Olivia, looked at Daniel, and shrugged his shoulders.

"What the hell's that supposed to mean?" said Olivia.

"That's my friend Eddie's way of saying he can't say," said Daniel.

"So, where do we go from here?" asked Olivia.

"I'm going to bed," said Armstrong, rising from his seat. "I suggest we pick this up over breakfast."

The policeman dropped twenty euro on the table and started to turn and leave.

Turning back to Daniel and Olivia, he said, "Try and get some rest tonight. Tomorrow we make plans for the end game."

Chapter Twenty-Seven

"Apparently, you are not hearing me, Mr. Churchill. It's over. You had your chance and you missed," said the voice on the phone.

"Missed? She wasn't even there," said Churchill. "Your man provided bad intel."

"It hardly matters," said the voice, too calm for Churchill's taste. "The entire situation must come to a conclusion. It's time to call it a day."

"Call it a day?" shouted Churchill. "And what about me?"

"Well, that isn't really my concern, now is it?"

Churchill gasped in disbelief.

"Go on holiday, Churchill. Nassau is lovely this time of year. Or maybe South Africa."

"And how am I supposed to do that?" asked Churchill. "I doubt seriously if I could cross any border at this point. Most of Europe must be looking for me by now."

"Pity," said His Highness. "Perhaps you should retire in Belgium. It's really quite nice there, once you get past the Belgians. Goodbye, Churchill."

At a small brasserie just down the street from their hotel, Olivia, Daniel, and Armstrong were making plans to bring this saga to a satisfactory resolution. At least, that was their intention.

As is his habit, the Chief Inspector was taking notes and drawing flow charts.

"Let's go over this again," said Armstrong. "You don't want to go public?" he said to Olivia.

"No, Eddie, you need to underline that or put a bunch of asterisks there. It's not that I don't want to go public . . . I absolutely insist that this never be made public. Nothing short of that is acceptable," said Olivia.

"I understand," said Armstrong. "And the same goes for the fact that you do not, under any circumstances, want to be a part of any discussion regarding succession."

"A whole bucket of asterisks there," said Olivia.

"Got it," said Armstrong. "Further, it is your wish to meet your brothers, but not your father, though I'm a bit unclear on that one."

"Let me try to make it clear," said Daniel. "Despite what Arthur Franklin said of the events that took place thirty years ago, my own research into the subject shows that fertilizing eggs and then destroying them wasn't just rare; it was absolutely unheard of. What Olivia's father did was out of desperation, and both Olivia and I believe that Diana was under great pressure to agree to it."

"On the other hand," Olivia cut in, "the semen that was provided must have been a willful act. It's not like Churchill grabbed some of Prince Charles' semen when he wasn't looking. That fact leaves me with an increasingly nasty feeling with every passing day. How could he have done that to this young woman? Even if it wasn't his idea, what kind of man would allow that?"

Olivia continued. "For whatever reason, I was obsessed with Diana from the very start, and it's clear to me that she was cruelly victimized from the day her marriage was arranged until the day she died."

Olivia drank some water and looked at Daniel with troubled eyes.

"The thing is, Eddie, at the end of the day, there are just a few things that MUST happen. Knowledge of all of this can only be extended to Susie Roberts, William, Harry, and Prince Charles," said Daniel.

"And Kate," said Olivia. "Where I come from, your brother's wife is your sister."

"Understood," said Armstrong. "But no one can make any guarantees once you've approached Mrs. Roberts."

"Of course, I realize that," said Olivia. "But since it is I who will be approaching Susie Roberts, then it is I who will have to make the judgment whether to take that chance or walk away."

"Walk away?" said Daniel, surprised by the statement.

"Yes, Daniel," said Olivia. "If I do not get the sense that Susie Roberts can pull this off, then you and I will simply disappear."

Daniel looked at his old friend, Eddie, and simply shrugged. Only Armstrong knew what that meant.

"Well, then," said the Chief Inspector, returning to his flow sheet. "It would seem that the next order of business is putting you in touch with the Roberts woman."

"No," said Olivia. "The next order of business is to stop yapping and eat. I'm famished."

Phillip Churchill had already walked a mile in his small hotel room in Luxembourg. He'd been pacing from one end to the other for over an hour like a tiger in a cage.

"No, this is wrong," said Churchill for the umpteenth time. "How can this be? How can they do this? This is wrong. It's wrong."

He stopped at the small clothes dresser and stared into the mirror that hung above it.

"This is wrong," he said to his reflection. "You are Lt. Colonel Phillip Churchill . . . defender of the crown . . . loyal servant to the House of Windsor . . . decorated officer of the 1st Battalion of the King's Regiment . . . a man of high honor and regard . . ."

Churchill slammed his right fist into the center of the mirror. With eyes the size of gold sovereigns, he stared at his shattered reflection.

"This is wrong," he said, yet again. "This cannot stand . . . this will not stand!"

In the pool of blood that was gathering on the top of his dresser, he traced the image of a crown with his left forefinger.

"This cannot stand," he said before wiping the crown from the dresser with side of his hand. "This will not stand."

In the staff lounge on the eighth floor of the John Radcliffe Hospital, Dr. John Wolsey, Nurse Margaret Osborne, and half a dozen close friends and associates of Olivia and Daniel were sharing their concerns and dismay over their missing colleagues.

"I think it's safe to assume they are together," said Wolsey. "Whatever is going on with Olivia, Daniel is trying to protect her."

"But what *is* going on with Olivia?" asked Christine Adams, who had been Olivia's roommate all through med school. "Who attacked her and why? Who killed her parents? What was all that craziness in the papers about an IRA plot?"

"I can tell you this," said Margaret Osborne. "I have called both Scotland Yard and the *Times of London* in recent days, and everyone I've spoken to has been so obviously evasive, it's as though they've all agreed to sweep this under the rug."

"Sweep this under the rug?" said Noreen Wentworth, a nurse on the Oncology Unit who worked side by side with Olivia every day. "How does one sweep something like this under the rug? People have been murdered. Olivia and Dr. Whittemore have dropped off the face of the earth. I have called, emailed, even handwritten letters to Olivia, and nothing. It's insane."

"We have to do something," said another doctor. "For whatever reason, Daniel and Olivia have gone underground, but someone must know where they are. Someone must be helping them."

"So what do you suggest?" asked Wolsey.

"We look for them ourselves," said Osborne to the approving nods of several of the others.

"Oh, come on, Margaret," said Wolsey. "Just how do you propose we do that?"

"The same way you look for anyone in this day and age," Margaret answered. "Google, British Social, Twitter, Facebook . . . how would you look for a long-lost relative or someone you went to school with? Come on, people. There's over a hundred years of higher education in this room."

A prattle of *yeses, okays,* and other affirmations rose up in the room.

"That's the ticket," said Terry Wentworth.

"Brilliant!" said Dr. Bishop.

"Let's do it," said several others.

"It's worth a try," said Wolsey, after a bit. "Let's make a plan of attack."

"Pardon me for interrupting," said Major Ripley, walking up to the table where Olivia, Daniel, and Armstrong were sitting. "I hate to be busting in on your little tea party, but if you three are going to make a habit of disappearing on me, I might as well go home."

Ripley glanced at Armstrong's scribbling and just shook his head.

"I'm afraid this is my fault," said Olivia. "I guess I'm a bit wary of the RMP since your boss tried to kill me and then murdered my parents."

"Olivia!" said Daniel.

"It's okay," said Ripley. "The lady does have a point."

"No, Major," said Armstrong. "The point is, we were wrong to exclude you despite what Churchill and Dixon did." And turning to Olivia, "This man saved my life, and I believe he is every bit as committed to doing what's right as was his friend, Major Wright. He is not our enemy Olivia."

Olivia took a deep breath and exhaled just as deeply.

"I hope you'll forgive me, Major. It's just . . . that my parents are dead, I miss them so much. I think about them all the time and the horrible way that they died."

Ripley watched as Olivia began to tear up; then he said, "It's Richard. Mind if I order something to eat?"

"Garcon!" said Olivia, Daniel, and Armstrong in unison.

Ripley just smiled as he pulled up a chair and joined them.

"There is something I need you to understand," said Ripley. "I cannot condone what Mr. Churchill has done, and I think Mr. Dixon made a very poor decision in joining him. Maybe Dixon wasn't given all the information, but it matters little. The point is, and I think I can speak for all the RMP senior officers; while we condemn the actions of Churchill and Dixon, it is not hard for us to understand them."

"I'm sorry. How does one understand the murders of innocent people?" asked Olivia.

Ripley looked at Armstrong to gauge his reaction.

"Let me," said the Chief Inspector. He turned to Olivia and hoped he got this right. "Olivia . . . we are all servants to the gods we choose, the moral beliefs we develop, our concepts of right and wrong, the codes we ascribe to, the oaths we make. You and Danny have pledged your lives to treat the sick and suffering . . . you approach life with an inherent optimism that the actions of good and decent people will make a difference. I happen to believe that, as well."

Armstrong shifted in his seat and stared at his friend Daniel. "When Danny and I came out of prep school in Surrey, we were faced, as are all young people of that age, with choosing paths. I chose to go into the military and ultimately to join the police. Along the way, I pledged allegiances, swore to uphold certain infallible principles—I made commitments to the law and to justice. You two also have certain unshakable tenets by which you live . . . and so does Churchill."

He looked at Ripley.

"The point is," said Ripley, jumping in, "for some of us, particularly in the military and in direct service to the crown, sometimes those things can become confused, conflicted, even warped to the point of irrationality. That, I believe, is what happened to Churchill and Dixon."

"But not to you?" asked Olivia. "Why?"

"Good question," said Ripley. "Maybe it's a matter of age and perspective, but I was raised and schooled to believe that blind allegiance has been at the root of some of the most hideous actions of humankind throughout our entire history. I guess what I'm saying is, it's one thing to serve, and quite another to serve without question."

"So who do you serve, Major Ripley?" asked Daniel.

Ripley pondered the question for just a moment.

"I serve the United Kingdom by protecting the Royal Family . . . even when they must be protected from themselves. That's where Churchill and Dixon faltered."

"Commissioner Richardson," said the Private Secretary on speakerphone. "I just want you to know that we've done about all we can on our end."

"I appreciate that, Mr. Secretary," said Sir Paul. "Thank you, Sir. I can only imagine what a sticky business this has been for you."

"No, Commissioner. You couldn't possibly imagine."

Chapter Twenty-Eight

It takes less than three hours to drive from Grenoble, France to Milan, Italy.

In yet another rented car, The Four Horsemen of The Apocalypse were readying themselves for customs and security for their flight to Gatwick.

"How much money do you have left, Danny?" Armstrong asked his friend, Dr. Whittemore.

"I'm okay," said Daniel.

"Good," said Armstrong. "Because there are a couple of civil servants here who are about tapped out."

"Gentlemen," said Olivia. "I don't imagine any of you are aware . . ." she had to pause to gather herself. ". . .due to certain unfathomable, hellish events that have recently beset me, you are riding in a car with a very wealthy woman."

All was quiet in the car for several moments.

"With the death of my parents, I have not only come into a considerable fortune in property, securities, life insurance and such, but the trust fund set up for me by my grandparents transfers entirely to me in one lump sum."

"Excuse me, love. I don't mean to be crude," said Daniel, "but, when you say wealthy, just what do you mean?"

"I mean that if it came right down to it, the four of us could rent cars, fly first-class, and stay in 5-star hotels for several hundred years," Olivia answered.

"Well, that may come in handy," said Daniel, putting his arm around Olivia and drawing her close to him.

"So Olivia," said Daniel, "have you given any thought to how you might use all that money, assuming we are not compelled to spend the rest of our lives renting cars and ordering room service?"

Olivia was silent for a few moments, then she spoke directly to Daniel.

"Dr. Whittemore," she began. "In March 2011, a number of extraordinary things occurred in my life—some tragic, some wonderful. First and foremost on the positive side of the ledger there is you, me and US. This, for Olivia Victoria Franklin, is a miracle so profoundly beautiful and amazing that it almost makes up for all the rest."

"Almost," said Daniel.

"Yes, love."

Olivia paused for a moment then continued.

"Daniel, the other day I was walking down the street with you, basking in the warm glow of our partnership, when a young boy . . . "

"Stop!" said Daniel. " . . . I think I know where you're going with this."

Armstrong and Ripley just looked at each other as though they were watching a play in the West End of London but somehow found themselves sitting on the stage as the actors played out the dramatic denouement.

"When you dashed out into the street . . . and when we were working there to save that boy's life among all the bystanders who were rummaging through their packages and handbags to find anything that could possibly help us, I felt her presence too . . . clearing landmines, hugging a child who was dying of AIDS, distributing food and medicine to the children of a nameless village in the middle of nowhere. I felt it, Liv. And that's what I saw for the rest of our lives."

Olivia burst out crying, drenching the shoulder of Daniel's jacket as though he had tapped a well in her soul.

"Are you alright, Dr. Franklin?" asked Major Richard Ripley.

"No," said Olivia. "But I've never been better."

It hadn't taken very long for the MPS to pick up Inspector Michael (Smitty) Smith. He had made no attempt to elude them—they found him in his home where he was paying bills and writing out instructions for his barrister.

Back at Scotland Yard, Smitty was calm, relaxed and mostly silent. Mostly.

"I'll tell you one last time," Smitty said to the police inspector who was questioning him. "I will only speak to Chief Inspector Armstrong."

A moment later the door to the interrogation room swung open and Commissioner Sir Paul Richardson entered the room.

"I'd like to speak with Inspector Smith privately," said Sir Paul, without even looking at the other Inspector. Smitty and the Commissioner were now alone.

"How are you holding up, Smitty?" asked the Commissioner. There was no response. "I understand," he continued. "I just want you to know that Eddie Armstrong is on his way back to London. Until he gets here, you don't have to answer any questions."

Smitty looked at Sir Paul but said nothing.

Sir Paul turned to leave, then said, "I'll have some food sent in or, if you prefer, we can move you to a room with a bed and you can get some rest."

"This is fine, Sir," said Smitty. "Thank you, Sir."

"Hello?" said Olivia's Aunt Helen after the fifth ring.

"Hi Aunt Helen, can you hear me?" Olivia said from a payphone in the loud airline terminal. "It's Livy."

193

"Oh, Livy, yes dear, I can hear you. Where are you, hon?"

"I still can't tell you that, Aunt Helen, but I'm okay."

"How okay can you be if you can't tell us where you are? *Thomas, pick up the phone. It's Livy.*"

"Hi, Liv. How are you?" said Uncle Thomas.

"I'm well, Uncle Thomas," she answered. "I'm under police protection, and I should be able to come home soon. I assume you've had the funeral," she said, her voice beginning to choke up.

"Yes, Liv," said Aunt Helen. "It was very moving. A lot of your friends from the hospital came, and there were several men from the Queen's Guard there, though I can't imagine why. What's that all about?"

"Yes, what's that all about?" her Uncle echoed.

"I can't explain that right now, but I should be able to soon," said Olivia. "I know you have a lot of questions, but you'll just have to bear with me for a while longer. I promise to tell you everything as soon as I can," she said, knowing it was a lie. "I have to get off now. Sorry. Talk to you soon."

Olivia burst into tears and turned away from Daniel, who'd been listening to her side of the call.

"I guess that's the essential truth, isn't it?" she said to Daniel. "If I want this to remain a secret, I can never tell anyone, not even my closest family and friends. I have to lie to the whole world."

"I don't see it that way, sweetheart," said Daniel, placing his hands upon her shoulders and spinning her around. "You didn't create this situation, but you are in the position and certainly have the right to control it to whatever extent you choose. Your life is your own Olivia—no one else's—and I think you're doing the right thing."

"Oh, Daniel," she said as she threw her arms around him. "I don't know what I'd do without you."

"And I pray you never have to find out," he said, stroking her hair.

"She's certainly a fine looking craft," said Ansell, a strapping young man who knew as much about boats as any man in the marina. "And all I have to do is ferry you across to Brighton?"

Ansell thought about it for a minute, studying the man's face. "You in some kind of trouble?" he asked, staring at the man's black eye. Obviously he had recently been in a fight.

"Nothing that can't be fixed by a cruise across the Channel," said Churchill, pulling out a hefty wad of bills.

Chapter Twenty-Nine

The easyJet flight from Milan to London's Gatwick airport is quick, efficient and cheap. There aren't a lot of frills, but nowadays most European travelers are more interested in just getting to where they're going in the least amount of time. In the minds of some, ease of travel is the only good thing about the European Union.

After dropping Daniel, Olivia and Ripley at a small hotel on the Bayswater Road, Armstrong went straight to Scotland Yard. Though Churchill was whereabouts unknown, a contingent of MPS and RMP personnel was organized to give Daniel and Olivia round-the-clock protection.

Upon arriving at Scotland Yard, Armstrong was told the Commissioner wanted to see him straightaway.

"Nice time in France?" said Sir Paul.

"France can be quite treacherous this time of year. Personally, I don't think you can top England in early April. Don't you agree?"

"Actually, we had a bit of a hailstorm . . . did I say hailstorm? I meant . . ."

"Yes, I can imagine," said Armstrong.

"Interesting," said Sir Paul. "I said that very thing to the Queen's Private Secretary, and he said I couldn't possible imagine. I expect he's right, given that I know so very little, Chief Inspector."

"You are a fortunate man, Sir Paul. There are certain things in this life of which it is best to remain ignorant."

"A sentiment shared by Inspector Smith, who is downstairs, eagerly awaiting an audience with you."

"Well, then I best not keep him," said Armstrong, rising from his seat.

Before he got to the door, he was offered a bit of advice.

"Eddie," said the Commissioner. "I've given you quite a bit of rope in this matter. See that you don't hang yourself or anyone else in this department."

"Understood, Sir."

"Well this seems nice enough," said Daniel of their two-room suite.

"Yeah, it's great, if you don't mind the armed guards out in the hall-way," said Olivia.

"And I definitely do not," said Daniel. "I could do with some time not looking over my shoulder every two seconds or planning our next move."

"Oh, Daniel, this is all insane," said Olivia before flopping on the bed. "Here we are, back in London, not safe and still hiding. All I want to do is call every single person I know and tell them that I'm okay and everything will be back to normal in a couple of days, but I can't. I want to call Terry Wentworth, my oncology nurse, and ask her how Peter's doing after his bone marrow transplant. I want to go home and sleep in my own bed and eat the tangerine sorbet in my freezer. Damn it, Daniel, this is so crazy I can barely breathe."

Daniel went over to the bed and sat beside her. He didn't say any-thing at first—he just sat with her.

"Come on," he said, grabbing her hand and pulling her upright. "We need to get some air."

"Where are we going?" asked Olivia.

"Out," said Daniel, who grabbed a sweater out of her bag. "I need to stretch my legs."

Daniel opened the door to their suite and told Constable Winthrop that the two of them were going for a walk.

"Uh . . . hmm," said the Constable.

"Call Armstrong and tell him that Daniel and Olivia need some alone time in the park," said Daniel before he and Olivia scooted down the hall and into a stairwell.

Armstrong walked into the holding room where Smitty had been for most of the day, and sat down at the table across from him.

The two men just stared at one another for a time.

"So?" said Armstrong.

"I'm sorry, Eddie. I didn't feel I had any choice," said Smitty.

"Care to explain?" said Armstrong.

"Ah, hell!" said Smitty getting up and knocking over his chair in the process. He paced around the room; finally staring at the large mirror that he knew was two-way.

"Not in here," said Smitty.

Armstrong understood.

"Open up," said Armstrong in a loud voice. "Let's go for a walk Smitty," he said putting a hand on the shoulder of a man he had long considered a friend.

They walked out of the interrogation room and down the long hallway that led to the main entrance of the building.

"Uh, excuse me, Chief Inspector," said a constable at the desk by the entrance to the building. "I don't believe this man is allowed to leave the building, Sir."

"It's okay, Rogers, we'll be back shortly. We have to pick up some more rope for Commissioner Richardson," said the Chief Inspector, to the utter consternation of the constable.

Hyde Park is just a minute from the Shaftesbury Hotel where Daniel and Olivia were staying. As Daniel steered her in to vast expanse of lawns, gardens, walking paths and statuary, Olivia looked back several times to see if any of Armstrong's or Ripley's men were following. She saw nothing.

"Daniel, kiss me quick!" said Olivia.

He did so without hesitation—a long, deep, passionate kiss.

"You know, it's okay to do that in Hyde Park," said Olivia.

"Actually, that was way beyond okay, sweetheart," said Daniel.

The two of them strolled arm-in-arm on a sunny, spring afternoon, and suddenly Olivia felt better.

"You are an amazing man, Dr. Whittemore," said Olivia.

"I am a man in love with an amazing woman," said Daniel.

"It's true that we are stronger and better together," she said. "We should always remember that."

"Not just remember," said Daniel. "We need to be forever grateful for the gifts we've been given, and we must use those gifts and the power of our partnership and love to ease suffering and make the world a better place."

"That's sounds pretty altruistic, don't you think?" said Olivia.

"No more so than Diana's passion for helping children and ease suffering in Africa and Asia."

"You're right, Daniel. Whether it was fate or destiny or the alignment of stars and planets that brought us to this moment, we cannot take for granted the circumstances of our lives. We are who we are; our love is a miracle; we must do our very best in all our endeavors."

"Olivia, kiss me quick," said Daniel.

Armstrong and Smitty were walking down Broadway, just a block from Scotland Yard.

"I have a pretty good idea what happened—I just have a couple of questions," said Armstrong.

"I'll tell you what I can, Eddie," said Smitty.

"Did you receive or were you promised any money?" Armstrong asked him.

"Of course not," said Smitty. "I'm not a mercenary."

"Can you tell me who contacted you?"

"No. I'm afraid I cannot," Smitty answered.

"Is that because you were contacted directly by a member of the Royal Family?"

Smitty said nothing.

"If you had been contacted by someone doing the Royals' bidding, what would you have done?" asked Armstrong.

Smitty stopped walking and turned to look at Armstrong.

"That's really what it comes down to, isn't it?" said Smitty.

Armstrong just returned his gaze.

"Well, let's put it this way, Eddie. If the Commander of the Royal Military Police, or the head of MI6, or the Prime Minister himself had asked me to do what I did, I would have given them the same answer as you."

"Which is?" asked the Chief Inspector.

Again, Smitty was silent. He turned and continued to walk.

After a bit, he asked Armstrong a question.

"Tell me, Eddie . . . what would you have done had the call come to you?"

"Thank god, it didn't," said Armstrong.

🐾

There were a lot of people in the park that afternoon. Though winter is relatively mild in London, with little or no snow most years, it is the longest, coldest, dreariest weather experience you will ever know. As such, spring is a celebration, as the city goes from abysmal to joyous.

"So we will figure out the best way to enlist the aid of Mrs. Roberts, and come what may, we will put our plan in motion to heal the sick and comfort the suffering, one child at a time," said Daniel.

"I can think of nothing more satisfying to do with my life than just that," said Olivia. "Thank you, love. I know you are giving up a great deal to do this with me."

"No, sweetheart. I am giving up nothing and gaining everything."

Daniel held Olivia close to him as they approached Hyde Park Corner. Neither of them was aware of the man on the motorbike who jumped the curb and sped up behind them. As the man reached over his shoulder to pull something from his backpack, Daniel suddenly turned and pushed Olivia onto the grass just before the bike struck him.

Like so many of the bystanders who witnessed the event, Daniel was shocked to see the cyclist lying on the ground, ringed by four men pointing guns in his face.

Daniel and Olivia just looked at each other. Thank goodness Danny escaped injury Olivia thought.

About three miles out from the Brighten Marina, Churchill, who was sitting aft, called Ansell to look at something.

"I can't tell what it is, but we are definitely dragging something," Churchill shouted.

"I don't feel anything," said Marcel, who was at the wheel.

"It might be a fishing net," said Churchill. "It's pretty close to the prop."

Ansell slowed the boat and walked aft to take a look. As he leaned over the gunwale to see what was doing, Churchill fired two shots into the back of his head, pitching Ansell over into the sea.

He walked calmly back to the wheel, laid on the throttle, and continued on the pre-set course to the Brighton Marina. As he focused on the lights ahead, he sang an old sea shanty . . .

My clothes are all in pawn
Go down you blood red roses, go down
And it's mighty draughty around Cape Horn
Go down you blood red roses, go down

Chapter Thirty

"Thank you all for coming," said Sir Paul Richardson to the six men gathered in his office. Present at the meeting were Chief Inspectors Jones, Anderson and Wentworth, along with RMP Majors Ripley, Blackstone and Townsend. Richardson introduced the men to one another.

"For those of you who don't know," Richardson continued, "Major Blackstone has been named Acting Commander of the Royal Military Police, and heading up things up on our end is Chief Inspector Armstrong, who is currently indisposed. Major Blackstone?"

"Sir Paul, Chief Inspector Armstrong and I met earlier this morning," said Blackstone. "This . . . what is this? This joint task force has been organized in response to a request from the highest authority."

"As you all know," Blackstone continued, "the former commander of the RMP has gone rogue, along with his predecessor, Mr. Dixon, who is now dead. We don't know where Churchill is or what his intentions may be, but we have to assume he is still on his deadly mission, which has already claimed the lives of respected colleagues from both of our services, as well as a number of innocent people. While all of you have some of this information and, no doubt, have heard rumors about the involvement of others who I will not name, it is our job to ensure the safety of Doctors Franklin and Whittemore, and to apprehend or otherwise neutralize Phillip Churchill."

"I'm a little confused," said Chief Inspector Wentworth.

"As well you should be," said Sir Paul. "You've been told nothing of Churchill's motive—nothing about who he is working for—and it might surprise you to know that neither Mr. Blackstone nor myself has that information, either."

The consternation on the faces of the officers was palpable.

"The point is that this is a need-to-know operation, and no one beyond a handful of people who are in possession of all the facts needs to know anything," said Blackstone.

"It should be noted that success in this undertaking will be measured by how well we do in making the whole affair appear that it never happened," said Sir Paul. "Are we clear?"

All present nodded in agreement.

Daniel and Olivia were sitting in Armstrong's office reviewing the Chief Inspector's latest flow chart.

"Well, I think that covers everything," said Armstrong, reaching for the phone.

"Do it," said Olivia, who promptly crossed her fingers.

Armstrong glanced at his notes and then punched in the number that was written in the margin of his notes.

"Good morning. Is this Mrs. Alexis Roberts? . . . This is Chief Inspector Edward Armstrong of the Metropolitan Police Service . . . I must speak to you about a matter of great urgency, and what I'd like you to do is look up the main number of Scotland Yard and call me at that number to confirm I am who I say I am . . . yes, Chief Inspector Edward Armstrong . . . very good. I'll await your call. Thank you Mrs. Roberts."

"How'd she sound?" asked Olivia.

"A little surprised, but not overly so," said Armstrong. "I suspect that since developing a friendship with Prince William, this sort of thing is not completely out of the ordinary for her."

"That's about to change, isn't it?" said Daniel.

Armstrong was about to respond when his phone rang.

"Chief Inspector Armstrong . . . yes, thank you. I apologize for the cloak and dagger, but this involves a matter so delicate that I must ensure we proceed with great caution . . . yes, I imagine you would . . . well, quite simply, I need to arrange a meeting between you and a Doctor Olivia Franklin on a matter that involves Prince William . . . no, I'm afraid I can say no more over the phone . . . Dr. Franklin would be willing to meet you anywhere you wish, at a time of your choosing. I should tell you that wherever that is, there will a security detail to ensure your privacy . . . yes . . . yes, that's correct . . . yes . . . thank you, Mrs. Roberts. I'm sure that will be fine . . . you too."

Armstrong hung up the phone and looked at Daniel and Olivia, who seemed about to burst.

"Tomorrow. 10:00 a.m. at her home in Kent."

Though technically on unpaid leave, Inspector Smith was in the technical surveillance suite, running a variety of sophisticated computer programs.

As both Armstrong and Richardson understood, all the rules go out the window when a member of the Royal Family issues a monarchical order. It is, no doubt, what originally motivated Churchill and Dixon; it's why Churchill, if caught, would never be charged with any crime; it's the reason why Smitty was being sanctioned but still at work. Great pressure had already been brought to bear to keep the attack on Olivia at the hospital, the death of her parents, and subsequent events, off the radar for most citizens—it is a singular characteristic of the Brits, which no other society shares.

Smitty was running trace programs on all phones that Churchill was known to have used, including the one that Smitty himself had texted several times. He was also monitoring all points of entry into the United Kingdom, so far with no results.

Though the whole world has become familiar with the technical wizardry of the computer magicians on television from NCIS, 24, CSI and so forth, in the real world it takes more than a few clicks of a mouse to find someone. Nevertheless, no country in the world had more surveillance cameras mounted in its public places than Great Britain, and Smitty was utilizing this intelligence resource to an extent never been seen before.

For over a year, he'd been writing a computer program that would utilize top-of-the-line facial recognition software to interface with every camera on every street corner, park, plaza, airport, train and Underground station on the grid. If Big Brother was being watched by his Bigger Brother, Smitty believed he just might find Churchill, should he happen to be in England.

"Come on, Duke," Smitty said to his computer, which he had named for the Duke of Edinburg, the foremost dispassionate watcher on the planet.

Olivia and Daniel were back at the Shaftsbury Hotel, discussing Olivia's impending meeting with Susie Roberts. They had already composed a carefully worded statement stating that Olivia was forever renouncing any claim to royal succession. The document would be notarized and witnessed by high-ranking members of Parliament before the end of the day. They were also discussing strategies that Olivia might employ to enlist Susie Roberts' help in acting as a go-between to Prince William.

"Pardon me while I freak out just a bit," said Olivia. "I'm just not comfortable with any of this strategizing."

Daniel watched her pace around the room before walking over to her and taking her hands in his.

"You're right, sweetheart. This is nuts," he said to her. "We are trying to calculate, plan, and rehearse what really needs to be a frank conversation between two women. I suspect we are guilty of over-thinking this, and that's all wrong. You will go and meet her, say what you will say, and the rest we should leave to the angels."

"Thank you, Daniel," said Olivia as she placed her arms around his shoulders. "I was getting very worked up and I didn't know why. As usual, you have brought me back to earth and helped me regain my perspective. God knows I love you so," she said, before kissing him.

Smitty was so busy staring at the banks of monitors mounted on the wall in front of his computer console that he didn't even notice Armstrong enter the room. The Chief Inspector stood at the back of the dimly lit suite, looking at what appeared to be rapidly changing images on security cameras—hundreds of images per minutes flashing across a score screens.

"Is that the sidewalk outside of Harrods?" he asked.

"It was," said Smitty as the screen switched to the Earl's Court Underground station.

"What is it you're looking for?" Armstrong asked.

"I'm not really looking for anything," said Smitty. "I'm watching Duke do his thing."

One of the monitors froze and zoomed in on a man in a crowd of people at Victoria Station and then moved on to a shot of Piccadilly Circus.

Armstrong moved to a nearby office chair and rolled over next to Smitty.

"So, how are you doing, my friend?" he asked Smitty.

"Much better," Smitty responded. "I am incredibly relieved and, quite frankly, I'm still in a state of shock that I'm here and not in jail."

"I would imagine so," said Armstrong. "But, the fact of the matter is that you are guilty of nothing more than zealous loyalty. At no time did the commissioner think otherwise. As for me, I believe that at this moment in time there is no more loyal member of this service than you."

"Thank you, Eddie. You have no idea what that means to me," said Smitty.

There was a loud beeping sound, and suddenly every monitor was focused on a shadowy image of a man exiting the Brighton Marina.

"What's going on?" asked Armstrong.

"Duke seems to think that's Churchill leaving the Brighton Marina," Smitty answered.

"Oh, come on," said Armstrong. "You can't even see the man's face."

"I'm working on that," said Smitty.

Armstrong got up from his seat and walked to the back of the room to take a call on his cell phone.

"Armstrong . . . yes, Chief Inspector."

There was a long pause while Armstrong was being briefed on a report that had just come into the Yard. The details were somewhat sketchy, but very much of interest to the Chief Inspector.

"Thank you, Mr. Wentworth," said Armstrong before ending the call. He strolled over to Smitty's position to fill him in on what he had just learned.

"I'm listening," said Smitty who was franticly tapping on the keyboard of his computer. There were all sorts of actions on the monitors before him—a wide assortment of angles, zooms, and enhancements of the image that had gotten Duke's attention.

"A body was found that washed ashore just south of the Brighten Marina—two shots to the back of the head," Armstrong said just as all the monitors simultaneously locked on the image of a man with wild and crazy eyes.

"Well, I'll be damned!" said Armstrong.

Chapter Thirty-One

It's less than a 90-minute drive from Central London to the beautiful county of Kent. Widely known as "The Garden of England," Kent is a quilt of orchards and hop gardens amid a series of ridges and valleys.

Daniel and Olivia could have taken the train from Victoria station, but they were craving alone time, something they had not been getting enough of lately. Though their car was being followed by RMP and MPS officers and tracked on GPS by Smitty, they enjoyed a modicum of privacy that they did not have in their heavily guarded hotel room or as they strolled the streets of London.

Back at Scotland Yard, the "Task Force" was in a strategy session to lay out their plans for the coming days and weeks. The principal concern was the apparent return of Phillip Churchill, whom they regarded as a threat to not just Daniel and Olivia, but to every living soul in England.

"I see no other way," said Chief Inspector Jones of a proposed plan to use Daniel and Olivia as bait.

"I'm afraid I have to agree," said Major Blackstone, despite his grave concerns.

"If there's another way to do this, I surely don't know what it is," said Chief Inspector Armstrong. "We don't know where Churchill is, but it's a sure bet he's looking for Olivia."

"So, how shall we go about this?" asked Major Ripley. Armstrong looked to Blackstone for suggestions.

"Well, we may not be the greatest detectives in the world," said Blackstone, "but the RMP are pretty adept when it comes to protecting our charges. The trick here will be to out-Churchill, Churchill. He'll be expecting a trap, anticipating diversionary tactics—he'll be looking for a singular opportunity to strike. Major Townsend, would you explain to the Inspectors the RMP concept of 'the moment of lethality?'"

Townsend rose from his chair and began pacing around like a college lecturer. As the lead tactician for the Royal Military Police protection details, Townsend was one of the foremost experts on the subject anywhere in the world.

He explained that the so-called "moment of lethality" was a concept developed by the British, the Israelis and the Americans after the assassination of President Kennedy. For just a moment in Dallas on Friday November 22, 1963, a man with a rifle was able to get off several shots from an upper floor window of the Texas Book Depository, killing the President of the United States, who was riding in an open car.

"Had planning for that event been based on MOL," Townsend explained, "three variables that were present that day would have been eliminated:

1. The President would not have been riding in an open car, something no other U.S. President has done since that day.
2. That building would have been emptied or sealed.
3. The weapon, a mail order rifle, would not have found its way into the hands of the shooter.

When we plan for something like that, we are constantly looking for holes in our protective scheme that would allow for such a moment of lethality."

"But one certainly cannot guard against every possible threat," said Chief Inspector Anderson.

"No, one cannot," said Townsend. "The idea is not to eliminate every conceivable threat—that would be impossible. The idea is to make a possible threat difficult to carry out successfully. Oswald was shooting at fish in a barrel."

"In a matter of weeks," said Blackstone, "there is going to be a Royal Wedding in London. There are those who would like to disrupt that event or even kill a member of the Royal Family. That's why, for the past months, the RMP has been going over every inch of the processional, every moment of scheduled events, every person who will be in attendance, everything that can be anticipated. This is not to say that an incident isn't possible. We are merely suggesting that anything that might be attempted will be extremely difficult to pull off."

"So, what we have to do, if I understand this," said Armstrong, "is to present Churchill with such an opportunity, without him realizing it's a trap."

"That is correct, sir," said Major Blackstone.

"And can we do that and ensure Olivia's safety?" asked Armstrong.

"No," said Townsend. "We can do that with an acceptable degree of risk to Olivia."

Daniel was sitting in the rental car just down the street from Susie Roberts' home, encouraged by the fact that Olivia had been inside for such a long time—and crazed by the fact that Olivia had been inside for such a long time.

He got out of the car to stretch his legs and was immediately surrounded by constables and RMP officers.

"Would you like to go for walk?" asked RMP Captain Nelson.

"You mean just the six of us?" asked Daniel.

"I can call for more officers if you'd like," said Nelson.

"I'm not sure the sidewalk is wide enough," said Daniel. "Perhaps I should remain in the car."

"Perhaps that would be best," said Nelson, leading him back to the rental.

Just then Daniel saw Olivia emerge from the residence, lean in to hug Susie Roberts, and walk to the car, surrounded by six other police officers.

"We'll be going back to the hotel now," Daniel told Captain Nelson.

"What an amazing coincidence," Nelson said with a smile.

"So?" said Daniel as Olivia fastened her seatbelt.

"So, drive," she answered.

Daniel started the car and drove slowly around the corner back towards the M20 to London.

"God, I'm exhausted," said Olivia.

"Can you tell me about it?" Daniel asked her.

"She's an amazing woman," said Olivia. "I like her very much."

"You know that I'm dying to hear every detail," said Daniel.

"I know, Daniel. I'll do my best."

Olivia used the entire ride back to London to tell Daniel of her conversation with Susie Roberts. Despite the most unusual circumstances of their meeting, they did not begin by talking about anything substantive. When she went in, Susie offered her tea, which she accepted. Then the two of them talked about the beautiful spring weather, her girls, who, like all kids, were delighted to be playing outside and enjoying their spring football leagues, and about her husband, Lex.

Alexis "Lex" Roberts sounded like a truly extraordinary man. He was the kind of strong, centered, self-assured individual who naturally attracted others because of his confidence and leadership. This was what made him such an exceptional military officer, something that was noticed from the day he signed on to serve his country. Major Roberts didn't have to go to Afghanistan. In point of fact, he had to transfer from one battalion to another in order to serve there. He died riding in the point vehicle of a caravan he was leading back to the Kandahar base after a successful engagement with the Taliban.

It had probably been the better part of an hour before the purpose of Olivia's visit became the focus of their conversation. Olivia began by telling Susie who she was—at least, who she was from her birth until March of 2011. At that point she felt she had established enough of a rapport to outline the events of the previous week.

What she shared with Susie Roberts sounded like something out of a suspense novel. Even as she heard the details come out of her mouth, she could hardly believe it. She spoke of the attack at John Radcliffe Hospital, finding out about the circumstances of her birth, Churchill, the murder of her parents, Paris, and so forth. Enough of the information would be verifiable, should anyone care to check it. She didn't feel that Susie Roberts would.

Olivia also explained to Daniel that she had spent a good deal of time trying to convince Susie that she wanted nothing from her biological family other than to make them aware of her existence and, if they so chose, to meet her brothers. She gave her the letter she and Daniel had composed, renouncing any claims to titles, property, succession and so forth. She also gave her another letter which she had written to her brother William, which she asked Susie to deliver personally when she saw him at the upcoming wedding just a couple of weeks away.

"Do you think she believed you?" Daniel asked her.

"I do," said Olivia. "Not only do I think she believed me, I think she is determined to convince Prince William that I am who I say I am. She asked me any number of questions designed to give her details that would prove my case, and then she did something extraordinary."

"What's that?" Daniel asked.

"She asked me for a lock of my hair."

Chapter Thirty-Two

Churchill walked quickly from the self-storage unit he kept near Waterloo Station, seeing no one who might be following him. The heavy canvas duffle bag he was carrying went back to his earliest days as a soldier. It contained, among other things, his service sidearm and the rifle he had used to qualify as an expert marksman. He knew he was taking a chance by going there to retrieve it, but it was unlikely that the existence of this space appeared in his dossier, and he didn't recall ever telling anyone about it.

He walked down the stairs to the Underground and caught a train that would take him to the small hotel he had checked into in Greenwich. He'd been working the plan in his head all day, and his confidence was growing. If Olivia was in London, he would soon accomplish his mission, and that would be the end of it. He would only need his two most prized weapons—one for Olivia, and one for himself.

Armstrong and Blackstone had just wrapped up their final planning session for what they were calling "Operation Smelly Cheese" and were standing on the steps of Scotland Yard.

"Do you think this is really going to work?" Armstrong asked the Major.

"If you want to catch a mouse, you set a mousetrap," said Blackstone. "If you want to catch a particularly pesky mouse, you set a hundred mousetraps."

And that's exactly what this operation was all about. The following morning, many dozens of RMP officers and an equal number of MPS officers would be baiting mousetraps all over London. Logistically it was a plan that bordered on art. Practically speaking, it was their best hope to "Out-Churchill, Churchill."

The plan was simple in concept, if difficult in execution. Plainly put, they would try to lure Churchill to any one of a number of spots that he might choose to make his move, and have half a dozen shooters there when he arrived. If Churchill could be anticipated, they would have him.

Daniel and Olivia were sequestered in their hotel room with more guards than a rap star at an awards show. They weren't happy about their situation, but they understood it.

Major Ripley was briefing them on the next day's plan, while trying to instill in them a level of confidence that was probably a bit more than the nature of the situation could reasonably sustain.

"So, just to review the main points," said Daniel. "You are certain that Churchill is in England."

"Ninety-nine percent," said Ripley.

"And if he's here, it's because he's going to try again to kill Olivia."

"If he's here, that's why," said Ripley.

"And you and Armstrong think you can catch him if Olivia and I are strung out like tethered goats to attract prey."

"Well, I wouldn't put it that way," said Ripley. "More like the mechanical rabbit at a dog track."

"And that's supposed to be reassuring?" said Olivia.

"Have you ever seen a greyhound actually catch the rabbit?" said Ripley.

Daniel and Olivia just looked at each other.

"So, I guess that covers it," said the RMP Major, rising from his chair. "You will be picked up at 8:00 a.m. and escorted to Scotland Yard."

"Okay," said Daniel, getting up and walking Ripley to the door.

"Uh, Richard?" said Olivia as the Major was about to leave. "Let's just say, for argument's sake, that there is a particularly gifted greyhound that actually catches up to the rabbit . . . what then?"

"Well, should such a thing happen, I can assure you there will be a hundred spectators on hand to splatter that doggie all over the track."

Churchill sat in his room in Davenport House in Greenwich, oiling his guns, checking his munitions and going over his plan. He was pretty sure he could predict the RMPs' every move. He was less sure about going head-to-head with Armstrong.

"You can do this," he said to himself. "You will do this!"

He carefully checked his weapons, yet another time, and placed them back in his duffle bag. He then dropped to the floor and did some push-ups before pouring himself a couple of drams of cognac.

Glass in hand; he walked over to the mirror above the bureau.

"This will end tomorrow," he said to his reflection. "This must end tomorrow!"

Churchill stared at his reflection in the mirror, and a raging river of thoughts passed through his head. It was as if he was being bombarded by everything he'd ever been taught, everything he had held sacred throughout his career, every oath he'd ever taken; he was stunned by any fleeting thought of the betrayal that had befallen him. In a sudden moment of delusionary clarity, he saw the crown with Excalibur stabbed through its heart.

"No!" he shouted. "This will not stand. This must not stand."

Churchill balled his right hand into a fist, drew it back to the fullest extent that his arm would allow, and violently thrust it toward the mirror, stopping just short of the glass.

"No!" He shouted. "This will not stand. This must not stand. Tomorrow I will draw this sword and order will be restored to the realm."

In the darkness of their bedroom at the Shaftsbury Hotel, Daniel and Olivia found warmth and comfort in their naked bodies entwined like a braided candle.

"You know that everything is going to be alright, don't you?" Daniel asked Olivia.

"I know it some of the time—maybe most of the time," she answered. "When we are together like this, or just holding hands when we're walking down the street, or when you look into my eyes, I know that we will always be alright, that nothing can touch us."

"But?" said Daniel.

"But when I think about all that has happened—when I think about my parents being murdered and out of my life in a moment—when I think about Diana in that tunnel, that same tunnel that we almost died in—the utter insanity of it all, I get scared, and the uncertainty of life becomes ever so real."

Daniel didn't say anything right away. Instead, he gained illumination from the darkness of their room.

"It is all real," he finally said. "Every bit of it. The insanity, the depravity of people, the hope and better nature of those who, in my view, represent God's brilliant vision for humankind, and our implacable need to strive and grow and evolve to justify his creation—that's all real. We live to love, to find and tap into the perfect essence of who we are, to get up in the morning and make coffee."

"Let me ask you something," said Olivia, propping herself up in an elbow and staring at the man she could not see in the darkness but whose likeness was etched in her brain. "Why is it that in the most tea-drinking country in the world, it's only cops and doctors who need coffee to go about their business?"

"Come here," said Daniel pulling her on top of him.

Chapter Thirty-Three

Just after dawn the following morning, Churchill took up a position on the B323 overpass at Castle Lane, about three-quarters of a mile from Scotland Yard. He was much too far away to take a shot from there and perfectly situated to identify the best sniper positions surrounding the police headquarters. At a quarter till eight, he was pleasantly surprised to see through his binoculars that all of those positions were being filled by multiple snipers. There were two shooters each on the rooftops along Claxton Street, Broadway, and Tothill Street, and another six snipers hidden in trees in nearby St. James Park. The message couldn't be clearer.

At 8:20 a.m., a caravan of vehicles, including an armored personnel carrier pulled up to the main entrance. Churchill had to laugh at the foolishness of it all. There she was, plain as day in a bright yellow dress that stood out among the drab attire of the police surrounding her. Could they possibly be any more obvious?

A short time later Churchill could clearly see Olivia, Daniel, Armstrong and Blackstone exit the building and climb into a black SUV. Blackstone's presence made the whole charade make sense.

As the SUV made its way toward Olivia's aunt and uncle's house, there was little conversation in the car beyond some nervous chatter.

"Just so you know, Chief Inspector," said Olivia, "if this vest I'm wearing is supposed to make me feel safer, it is having the exact opposite effect."

"Well it wasn't designed to make you *feel* safer," said Armstrong. "It was designed to make you a smaller target."

"See, that's the thing," said Olivia. "It makes me feel like a target. The size doesn't really matter."

"Everything is under control," said Blackstone. "You are in no real danger today."

"Does that mean I'm in unreal danger today?" Olivia asked him.

"Only from Chief Inspector Armstrong's driving," Blackstone answered.

"Oh, that's reassuring," said Olivia.

"Well, that's our motto," said Armstrong. "To protect and reassure."

Armstrong picked up a hand-held radio and said, "Unit 2, please report." The voice of a senior officer came back reporting that there was nothing unusual within a four-block perimeter of Thomas and Helen Franklin's home.

"Maintain positions," said Armstrong.

Churchill was back in the car he had stolen the night before. He was headed to the John Radcliffe Hospital in Oxford to confirm his suspicions. Radcliffe is a sprawling campus of a dozen or more buildings. There is little concealment around most of the complex, which is ringed by car parks and open spaces.

At the far northeast end of the campus, well away from everything else, is the Osler Lodge, a high-rise building with a long view of the entire hospital complex. Using his binoculars from the roof of that location, Churchill counted no fewer than twenty-four snipers spread out across the various rooftops, all in prone positions looking through their high-mag scopes to view every person on campus.

"Pretty clever, Major Blackstone . . . but not clever enough."

⁕

"Can't we go in?" asked Olivia as the SUV pulled up in front of her aunt and uncle's house, but nobody moved.

"No, sweetheart. I thought that was clear," said Daniel. "We are just here to try and flush Churchill."

"Well, I don't care for this game," said Olivia.

Before anyone could stop her, Olivia was out the right rear door of the SUV. Two seconds later, Armstrong, Blackstone and Daniel were shielding her with their bodies.

"If it makes any difference," said Blackstone, "your aunt and uncle aren't home. We moved them out last night."

"Well, you might have mentioned that," said Olivia, turning and walking back to the car.

Inside the SUV, everyone took a few deep breaths.

"I apologize, gentlemen. I'm afraid my nerves are a little jangled today," said Olivia.

"We all understand that, Doctor," said Major Blackstone. "It's to be expected."

"Funny, I never expected any of this," said Daniel.

"Well, you always were a bit of a wanker, Danny," said Armstrong.

⁕

Churchill drove past Olivia's aunt and uncle's house just minutes after the SUV departed. He didn't have to get out of his car to detect the police presence. Apparently, Olivia had already been there, because the police and RMPs on station did little to conceal their presence.

"Shame on you, Major Gideon," he said upon seeing one of his former officers standing openly on the roof across the street from the Franklin's. "No pudding for you tonight."

Sir Paul Richardson had a nasty feeling about the operation that was underway. Unlike most of his predecessors, who were named to the position of commissioner as an awarded honor, regardless of qualifications, Sir Paul had been a policeman long before he was knighted. He'd also known Lt. Colonel Churchill for more than twenty years, and there was something about the op that was gnawing at him.

He walked down the hall from his office and took the elevator up to the Technical Services Division, where he found Smitty huddled over his computer console.

"How'd you manage that, Smitty?" he asked, referring to the bank of monitors which were cycling every three seconds between live shots from nearly a hundred cameras trained on every sniper position that was active at the moment.

"With these," said Smitty, holding up one of the many golf ball-sized cameras he had deployed on rooftops all over London.

Sir Paul just stared at the monitors in awe until his cell phone rang.

"Commissioner Stephenson . . . really . . . that's great. Tell him I'll be right down. Stay with it, Smitty, and keep me informed," said Sir Paul as he walked to the door.

At the Radcliffe campus, the task force was about to withdraw when a junior RMP officer came running over to Blackstone and Armstrong.

"Sir, I found these on the roof of that building over there," he said, pointing to the Osler lodge. He handed Blackstone a pair of military-issue field glasses.

"He's been watching the watchers," said Armstrong. "Seal the perimeter. I'm going to call in more people to conduct interior searches of all the buildings. And let's get her back to the Yard."

"Agreed," said Blackstone.

During his morning reconnoiter of Scotland Yard; Churchill had determined that the best sniper position was on the roof of the Allegro Con Brio Restaurant on Caxton Street. It was barely one hundred yards from the entrance, and it had an unobstructed direct line of sight.

Carefully making his way toward the roof, Churchill opened the door about an eighth of an inch to reveal a single sniper, his rifle on a tripod, just inches above the roof's edge. It was one of Armstrong's men, which was a lucky break.

Quietly placing his duffle bag down inside the door, Churchill took a few deep breaths and replayed the plan he'd been visualizing for hours.

"Is your radio down?" he asked the startled policeman as he walked quickly to his position.

As the sniper quickly rose to his feet, Churchill said something about it being a long day before slashing the man's throat, inflicting a fatal wound that killed him before he hit the tar and gravel surface.

Churchill dragged the man aside and took his position at the mounted rifle.

Smitty got up from the console and walked to a nearby table to refill his coffee cup. It had indeed been a very long day, and his eyes were weary from focusing on the wall full of monitors in the darken room.

Tapping a few commands on his keyboard, the majority of screens switched to cameras at John Radcliffe Hospital.

Long minutes went by while Churchill waited for his target to appear. He checked the calibration on the rifle's scope and adjusted for the changing winds several times. An incredible sense of peace and well being washed over him. He patted his service automatic, which was strapped to his waist. It felt very reassuring.

When the black SUV rolled up to the entrance, the adrenalin surge that coursed through Churchill's body was welcome and altogether expected. Sniper training had taught him to use that to his advantage by slowing his breathing and gently fingering the trigger of his weapon.

As her yellow dress emerged from the SUV, he waited for her to stand upright.

"It would be my great pleasure to separate your head from your shoulders," said a voice from behind, as the unseen intruder pressed the barrel of a gun against his neck and kicked at the stock of the rifle.

Churchill slowly rose and turned to see Nigel Prescott standing before him.

"Perhaps you will do me the honor of letting me end this myself," said Churchill, slowly moving his hand toward his holstered weapon.

Prescott fired a single shot into the center of Churchill's forehead.

"I think not," said the Inspector.

Chapter Thirty-Four

Daniel and Olivia woke up early, as was their habit. While Olivia showered and dressed, Daniel made coffee and a light breakfast, which he would serve on the veranda. The veranda, which was a screened-in porch, was their favorite part of the house. In the distance, one could just make out the sound of Victoria falls crashing into the Zambezi River.

Because of the altitude, the climate was quite mild year round. It seemed the ideal place for them to establish their clinic, as they were in easy reach of South Africa to the south, Botswana to the southeast, Zambia to the northwest, and Mozambique to the east. There was also the advantage of English being a widely spoken language—as a former Crown Colony; there was much about what once was Rhodesia that was still quite British.

Though Olivia had long been aware of the prevalence of pediatric cancer in the region, she did not fully appreciate the extent of the problem until she and Daniel arrived. In addition to the many autoimmune diseases arising from AIDS, Childhood Leukemia and Burkett's Lymphoma were also widespread throughout the region. The good news was that many of the diseases that afflicted children here were treatable, and in the case of Burkett's, benefitted from the surgical removal of tumors. Together, the pediatrician and the oncologist were an ideal team for tackling many of the medical problems of these children, though they were acutely aware that their skills and dedication would only go so far.

Still, in the lives of the children they were treating, Daniel and Olivia were the bearers of daily miracles. Nothing they had ever done in their careers was quite so gratifying.

"Dr. Princess, Dr. Princess," eight year-old George was shouting as he ran up to the house. "Oncles are here."

Oncles are what the village children called the aid workers from the International Society of Pediatric Oncology, the group that provided equipment and supplies to clinics such as theirs in several African nations.

"Thank you, George," said Olivia. "Please tell them we'll be there straightaway."

"Well, I guess I'd better get ready," said Daniel, rising from the table. "I won't be a minute."

Daniel started for their bedroom suite and then turned abruptly. "By the way, Dr. Princess, have I told you today that I love you very much?" He leaned over and kissed her before continuing to the shower.

"I love you too, Lt. Dan," she called after him.

Their nicknames have interesting stories behind them.

In 1993, Princess Diana visited Zimbabwe as part of a tour to survey the medical needs of the children in this part of Africa. Many of the women of the nearby village—mothers of the children they were now treating—were little girls who remember the blond-haired princess from that trip. When they first saw Olivia, they tagged her with the moniker 'Dr. Princess,' and it stuck. Daniel's nickname was somewhat less glamorous, deriving from a character from the movie Forrest Gump, which had only recently hit these parts.

While Daniel showered and dressed, Olivia cleared the dishes and put away the remaining food before checking her email.

Before leaving London, Daniel and Olivia bought satellite phones that would provide them with voice, data, and Internet anywhere in the world. With a USB connection into their laptops, the so-called *World Wide Web* was literally that.

Olivia had multiple email accounts, including one that appeared in a book about her in 2011, just after she disappeared. That one was populated mostly by readers who were obsessed with the clues that appeared in the book that might allow them to communicate with her. She enjoyed reading those emails, though rarely did she answer.

She also couldn't resist checking periodically with the Facebook pages and Twitter accounts associated with her disappearance. But mostly, she looked for messages from friends and family at oliviavfranklin@gmail.com.

🕸

"I got an email from Eddie Armstrong this morning," said Olivia, as Daniel wrestled the Land Rover over the pitted track that was the road from their home to the clinic.

"Really? What did he have to say?" Daniel asked.

"You mean, besides calling you a wanker?"

"Yes. Besides that," said Daniel.

"He said he is well, that he is looking forward to seeing us on Saturday, and that our friend, Richard Ripley, has been reassigned to the Duke and Duchess of Cambridge. Oh, he also said that he had to tell us something about Churchill."

"I wonder what he has to tell us?" said Daniel. "I am getting a uneasy feeling."

"Let's not think about Churchill," said Olivia. "I can't wait to see Harry, William and Kate again."

"Have you heard from anyone else?" Daniel asked.

"Margaret of course, she emails me almost everyday. I also heard from Janet Poole from SIOP, The International Society of Pediatric Oncology, a small contingent from the U.N., Uncle Thomas and Aunt Helen, Mugabe is sending some minister, which solves that problem, and get this - Bono is coming."

"Are you sure we're not taking too big a chance here," asked Daniel.

"No," said Olivia. "I think the plan is brilliant. The press will establish us as a pair of British Good Samaritans named Smyth-Pelly; photos will show a brunette and a guy with a shaved head wearing a surgical mask— it's a way to come out into the open and remain completely in the darkness. Don't you think you will enjoy it here more if you know we can go anywhere as Mr. and Mrs. Smyth-Pelly from Africa? Hell, it's been all set up by MI6—maybe they'll send Commander Bond to look after us?"

"God, you're cute," said Daniel.

When Daniel and Olivia arrived at the clinic, there was a line of twenty or so mothers and their children waiting for them. Many had traveled all night from other parts of northwest Zimbabwe.

There were no procedures scheduled for this day. Today was just about treatment and follow-ups. The clinic was still waiting on the delivery of radiological equipment from Switzerland. It was promised to be there before the dedication scheduled for next Saturday.

"Good morning, Doctors," said Gloria, an oncology nurse from Johannesburg whom Daniel and Olivia had recruited to serve as their Chief of Everything. Gloria worked fourteen-hour days, training men and women of the village to assist her in a variety of tasks. She was also the principal liaison to St. Anne's Hospital in Harare, where she and Olivia had set up a program with the Director of Nursing to provide students to do their fieldwork at the clinic.

As "Dr. Princess" and "Lt. Dan" approached the clinic, local children laden with fresh fruit and vegetables for their esteemed benefactors surrounded them. This was one of Olivia's favorite parts of the day.

"Unacceptable," shouted Big George, father of the younger George who had visited them earlier.

"This new generator will never work," proclaimed Big George, who was prone to make everything into a catastrophe.

"George," said Daniel, "Settle down. What's the problem?"

"Everything!" George shouted, waving his arms wildly above his head. He had said the same thing the day the clinic's truck didn't start because it had no gas.

"Settle, George," said Daniel. "What's up?"

George ran to the nearby diesel generator that had just been delivered, grabbed something, and quickly ran back.

"This is the problem," George shouted, handing Daniel the instruction manual.

Daniel looked at the book, smiled, and looked up at George.

"Well, I guess you'll just have to learn Japanese," he said.

"Ahhh," George shouted as he ran off into a nearby field.

Inside the clinic, which was almost finished though it had been in use for weeks, Daniel and Olivia took a moment to take it all in.

"We are so fortunate," said Olivia.

"Yes, we are," said Daniel, his arm around her shoulder, pulling her close as they gazed through the window at a beautiful world.

"Yes we are," she said, completely at peace.

The moment was broken by the piercing ring-tone of Daniel's satellite phone.

"Hello . . . yes, I understand."

Daniel took Olivia's hand in his.

"Come on," he said. "We have to get out of here, now!"

ABOUT THE AUTHOR

Nancy E. Ryan was a New York and New England media executive for 40 years. After accomplishing her goals in the media world, she decided to try her hand at writing.

Nancy now lives in Palm Beach Gardens, Florida with her husband Barry O'Brien and their two Bichon Frises, Nicholas and Alexander. **The Disappearance of Olivia** is her first novel.

Nancy engaged the talents of Alan Forray for **The Disappearance of Olivia**.

Alan is a writer, media consultant, and newspaper columnist with over thirty years of experience in journalism, entertainment, and education. He is a graduate of the Newhouse School of Public Communications at Syracuse University.

Nancy@NancyERyan.com